Murder is a Debate

By: Brandy Nacole

Brandy Nacole
www.brandynacole.com

Edited by Samantha Eaton-Roberts
Cover Design by Brandy Nacole

First Edition March 2019

Chapter One

The bell rang, causing Nora's nerves to twitch. Students eagerly jumped from their seats and rushed for the door. She took a breath and rummaged through her bag, letting everyone get a head start. The more people who left, the fewer she'd have to make small talk with.

"Hey, Nora, you ready for the debate tomorrow?" Of course. It had to be Stacey who waited for her. She was always trying to fish for news and drama. The girl lived off it.

"As ready as I always am." It was the standard reply. The same one she gave to Stacey every week. It was a wonder the girl even bothered at this point. Nora scooped up her book bag and headed for the door, keeping her head low. *Less eye contact equals less chat time.* That's what Charlie told her at their last Thursday meeting anyway. Nora hoped she was right. She needed to shake Stacey, pronto.

Her attempts were futile. Though she struggled and was a little winded, Stacey managed to keep up with Nora. "You going to practice today?"

Caught off guard by the question, she stumbled but managed to catch herself as she swiveled around to face Stacey. "What practice? It's Thursday." *This cannot be happening. It can't. Not today.*

"Yeah…" Stacey drawled, her eyes filling with concern. As Vice President, Nora should have been the first to know of a change. This time she had obviously slipped. "Didn't you get the group message?" As she asked, Stacey pulled out her phone. "You're in it." To emphasize that she wasn't lying, she held the phone out in front of Nora.

Aggravated, Nora gets her phone out of her bag. How could she have missed something like that? A message was splayed across the screen, but not the one Stacey was referring to.

Can't wait to see what creepy ass clues you come up with this time.

Nora's pulse quickened, and she shoved the phone back into her bag. "Must have missed it," she said dismissively. Stacey stood close as Nora began spinning the lock on her locker door. Stacey's eyes were trained on her with skepticism. Nora shoved her books inside with a little too much force. How was she going to get out of the debate meeting? No way was she going to miss an MM meeting. It was her turn to set the scene.

Stacey leaned up against the locker and started examining her cuticles. "Personally, I think we should cut Brittany from the lineup. I mean, come on, she has an A-minus average. She flopped at our last debate."

Nora's shoulders tensed as Stacey's condescending tone rolled over her skin. No wonder she had chosen her as the victim last time. "I think she's pretty good." Her remark was flat, her mind too occupied to come up with a believable excuse. Brittany wasn't a bad team member, none of them were. If they were, they wouldn't be ranked number one in the state.

At most schools, the debate club might not be important, but it was everything to their school. Northeast Pinewood Academy was known for many things, but its debate team was what many would consider the All Stars, especially if a debate member was also in volleyball, tennis, or golf. If someone was an athlete *and* on the debate team, they were a hot item.

Nora was not a hot item. She felt more like the debate team's sympathetic project. Ever since her sister's incident three years ago, nothing had been the same. Everyone's forced attempts to include her was so notable it made her sick. Never mind the fact that without her they would have lost their match last week. Yeah, let's treat her like the outsider.

"Whatever," was Stacey's response to Nora sticking up for Brittany. Typical Stacey response. "I've got to swing by my locker before heading to the auditorium. Want to walk with?"

Nora shoved her Algebra I book into her bag, her palms clammy. Her heart raced as she opened her mouth then shut it again. Sweat built on her brow and upper lip. *This is stupid. Just tell her no. What's she going to do?*

"Actually, I can't. I didn't know about the meeting and I've already made other plans." Nora's voice wavered but she maintained her resolve with the decision. As expected, Stacey's eyes went wide. Nora never skipped a debate meeting.

"You mean you're skipping practice. Seriously?"

Irritation crawled all over Nora. It shouldn't, but it did. It wasn't like she was asking for a whole lot. She was missing a practice, one practice. In the last two years, Nora had never missed a single practice, debate, or meeting. Not once. It shouldn't be as big of a deal as Stacey was making it out to be.

"Seriously," she snapped. "And if you or anyone else has a problem with that, I can sit out Saturday." The blood drained from Stacey's face. She knew what kind of hit the team would take if Nora didn't compete. They'd get slaughtered.

After giving Stacey her best fake smile, Nora turned on her heel and headed for the main exit. She felt lighter, almost free. She'd confronted people in her life, sure, but it was usually people she didn't know or someone online. Debates she could handle in person or online, but standing up for herself was a rarity.

As she hurried down the hall, she dug out her phone. "Crap," she mumbled and shoved the phone back into her pocket. She was going to be late.

A low whistle caught her attention right before she spotted them. Leaned up against their lockers were Reed Benson and Kyle Austin, two of the only students at the academy who could care less about their grades yet continue to get a full ride scholarship.

"Surprised you have something like that in you, Fletcher." Kyle smirked. "Didn't think being rude was in your nature."

Nora tightened her grip on the backpack straps to hide the fear tensing her body. Something about Kyle had always given her the creeps. Reed only seemed to follow along with him because there was no one else at the school who would give him the time of day when he transferred three years ago. She'd never seen them together outside school.

"You'd be surprised what people are capable of," she remarked, pleased she was able to keep the quiver out of her voice. Kyle laughed, making chills break out across her skin. Reed said nothing. As she rounded the corner toward the exit, she glanced back over her shoulder. Reed's eyes met hers for the briefest of seconds before he disappeared out of view. It didn't matter. She got the challenge in his eyes loud and clear. He was calling her bluff.

Nora's head swam from all the excitement as she pushed through the main entrance. With a greedy gasp, she sucked in the sweet, crisp air. Six months ago, she would never have talked to anyone like she just had Stacey or Kyle. Had she been confronted back then, she would have kept her mouth shut and tucked tail.

Maybe Liv and Charlie were right. Maybe the Murder Club was changing them.

~

"You're late," Liv said before shoving another Dorito in her mouth.

Nora slid into the chair across from her. "I don't want to hear it. You have no idea what I went through to get here." Okay, it wasn't all that dramatic. It's not like she got into a real fight or anything, but still. It wasn't a walk through the park, skip over the bridge, and grab a bag of chips at the corner store experience like they had on their walk over.

"Is our prep getting overwhelmed?" Charlie made sad puppy eyes at Nora before snagging another Dorito from Liv. Nora followed her lead and snatched one of her own. The cheesy flavor sent waves of comfort that she needed.

"I thought we were over this crap. I'm not your prep and you're not my home girls. We are just people with common interests, status aside." Nora prepped and pushed this mantra since first meeting the girls six months ago. Before that day, she never thought to hang out with two girls from the west side of town, let alone to solve fake murders with them.

They'd all met online, where status and appearance were nothing. People were hateful, nice, complimentary, or spiteful depending on their mood and a person's cause. Someone's status in society means nothing online. Nora knew that, which was why when Liv asked if she wanted to meet up in person once she discovered Nora was a local, she froze. Online Nora was like the rest of the people on Murder Chat. They were there to solve murders and create the next one. It was a lot like D&D, but with dead bodies and crime scene clues. The more someone chatted and solved, the more popular they became. Nora had become quite popular. Her solved crime rate was one of the highest in the group. Then Liv reached out to her. She wanted to take the debate offline and get more active. She wanted to meet in person, which meant Nora showing who she really was and having a dozen panic attacks before coming to that first fateful meeting at the library.

Charlie took another chip, to which Liv stuck out her tongue. The two went to school together at Center Valley High, where the football team was a solid two and the art department was shut down due to funding.

"The formal is next week. You want to hit the strip mall with us after this?" Charlie's bright hazel eyes peered at Nora with excitement and a drop of hope. The last time she'd invited Nora over to her house, three weeks ago, she'd tucked in her shell, mumbled an excuse, and hit the ground running. It wasn't that Charlie's mom's homemade salsa and tortillas sounded horrible, they sounded rather amazing; it was the prospect of having to hang out with them outside their meetings.

Again, Nora started to give a roundabout excuse, but stopped. If she was ever going to conquer life and become the FBI agent she hoped to be, she was going to have to start picking up on some social cues. She struggled with it, but she knew a moment when it presented itself. This was a moment, one she didn't need to pass up no matter how badly it terrified her.

"Sure, sounds fun." Once she said it, she was surprised to learn it didn't feel like a lie. A little excitement was actually starting to build. She couldn't remember the last time she went shopping offline.

Tossing the empty Doritos bag aside, Liv scooted up closer to the table. Her green eyes, framed by beautiful red hair, looked at Nora with anticipation. "What do we have this week, detective?"

Nora smiled. Now that the small talk was over, it was time to get down to business. Dragging out her flashcards, she settled down into her chair while Liv and Nora poised their pens over their notebooks, ready to take notes. Nora's nerves flared, as they always did right before she was about to present her crime scene.

"Jackson Ash, seventeen-year-old male." She paused and glanced down at her notes. The description she'd written last night was for Gary, the head captain on the debate team. Her victims were always from the debate team. Gary, with his perfect caramel complexion and accusing brown eyes, had called her out in front of the team yesterday for being thirty seconds late. *Thirty seconds.* Excuse a girl for starting her period. Case and point being, when she got home last night, still fuming over the incident and needing to write out the crime scene, she had easily chosen him. Problem was, it was a pattern they were sure to pick up on and question her about. Was she out to murder everyone on her team? Maybe, but for the sake of fun, she decided she needed to shake things up a bit. A new face appeared, and she hastily changed the description as she read it out loud.

"Light brown hair, five-eight, small build. He was found floating face down in the lake. There are laceration marks on his forehead, neck, and back. Autopsy reports indicate he died due to blunt force trauma, not drowning."

Liv looked up from her notes, her face now pinched and serious. It always got intense as they absorbed all the facts. "Dang. Dude took a beating."

Nora thought back to Kyle standing in the hallway today, a smirk on his face. Sometimes, the best way to let off some steam was to murder someone. Even if it was only pretend.

"Thought I would get a little more creative," she said with a shrug. "Gun shots and knife wounds were getting a little old."

Liv considered this. "True. So now we're going for blunt force trauma. Got it." Her pencil scratched across her paper, hard and fast.

"Suspects?" Charlie asked, her own pencil poised and ready. A thrill rushed through Nora. This was the best part.

She knew she was going to have to make some adjustments to accommodate the change in victims, but for the most part she kept the details the same. "Three suspects. David Evergreen, age eighteen, was last seen with the victim an hour before his cell lost signal. Sarah Pine, age twenty-one, was last seen arguing with the victim outside the 7-Eleven on Main Street. Last, Hazel Oak, seventeen, student at Eastside Cedar. Texts were discovered of her threatening the victim, with promises of torture before death."

Charlie slapped her hand on the table. "I choose her. It's obvious."

"You always go for the obvious ones," Liv argued. "I want to hear about the witnesses."

Nora smiled. Liv always wanted to hear about the witnesses. They were her first suspects. "Wes Maple stated he saw the victim leaving his home at 9:45 pm, which, according to the autopsy reports, was two hours before time of death. Wes stated Jackson was alone when he left his home." Nora flipped her notes over. "Mrs. Birch was the one to report the argument between Jackson and Sarah Pine. She stated Sarah looked rather rattled and tailed Jackson once he pulled out of the gas station."

"Evidence?" Liv prompted.

Nora smiled and handed over the file she'd made up. "You'll find everything you need to know in here."

Liv returned the smile, full of anticipation.

Chapter Two

Liv: That was a good case. Keep it up and we won't be able to crack the next one.

Nora smiled. That was the goal. She'd studied law, psychology, forensics, and criminal law for some of her elective online classes. She wanted to be good. She wanted to be damn good. State University wasn't going to take a slacker. Her dad made sure she understood that from day one of kindergarten. *Fletchers don't slack. We make sacrifices and get things done.* It would have been nice had her dad informed her her friends list would be nonexistent during the process.

Nora: That's the goal. ☺

She tossed her phone down on the desk and began rummaging through her backpack. She had exactly one hour and sixteen minutes to finish her algebra homework and start her history paper before her mother yelled it was time for dinner. She'd have to make small talk with her dad about her homework while her mother watched her with a critical eye. Though she and her mother weren't close, the woman was a walking lie detector. It's how she had earned her title as criminal profiler. That was until she had Nora and quit. Then Nora and her sister Beth became her constant case.

Her phone vibrated on her desk, startling her. She was still getting used to this friend business. No one texted her from school unless they needed a debate team update or had homework questions.

Liv: That dress you got. Amazing. You're going to look stunning.

Nora blushed. She still couldn't believe she'd bought the dress. A few compliments and she was digging out her credit card.

Nora: I don't know why I even bothered. I have nowhere to wear it.

Liv: Go to the formal with us. It'll be fun. You can be my date. ;)

Nora: I don't know. Won't you have a date?

Liv: High school boys are so immature, though Charlie will try to convince you otherwise.

Nora had never been to a dance. The few they'd had at the Academy, she'd never been invited by anyone, and going without a date was out of the question. It was considered in poor taste.

Nora: I'll think about it.

She put the phone away and got to work on her math. It felt like only minutes had passed when her mother eventually called to her from downstairs. *Show time.* As usual, her father was already waiting at the head of the table. It'd always been this way. Her mom would cook dinner, wait until her father got home, he'd put his things down and go straight to the table. Once he was seated, her mother would call for her and her sister to come down for dinner.

Nora had just sat down when Beth came trudging into the dining room. She looked rough, as if she hadn't slept in days. That's probably because she hadn't. Beth was on all sorts of medication to help control her anxiety and insomnia. Funny thing was none of it worked. Beth was still an anxious zombie who patrolled the house at night like a creeper off Minecraft. It was eerie. It was also Nora's fault.

"How have my girls been?" Her father looked at her expectedly. Beth's usual response was 'fine' as she stared down at her food. He wanted more than a one-word answer and therefore always turned to Nora for conversation.

She thought back to her day. It was all normal minus her skipping a debate meeting, going to a murder club meeting, and then buying a dress for no reason. She knew she didn't have to mention it until it showed up on her credit card statement. Even then, she may not be questioned on it. Her father may think it was her mother. Nora and Beth weren't in the habit of spending money, another lesson they had learned from their father. *Earn it, save it.*

Still, she wanted to mention it. She always talked academics with her family and that was it. "I bought a dress today after school."

Her father didn't look phased, but her mother did. "That's wonderful. Is there a special occasion?"

She thought of Liv's invitation to their school's formal. Their very public, and in her dad's eyes, poor school.

They'd flip their lid if they knew Nora was hanging out with girls from the outskirts of their high-end community. "No," she lied. "I just thought it was pretty. Maybe I'll have something to wear it to one day."

Her dad grunted. "Don't fret over such useless notions, Nora. You know where your focus should lie."

She knew all right. He pounded it into her head, daily. Beth grunted across the table and Nora snapped up her eyes to meet her sister's. A tear ran down her cheek as their gazes locked. Beth was always sad, but today she looked even worse. Nora's stomach flopped. She knew the sadness wasn't for herself. Beth was sad for Nora, and she hated it. She hated sympathy of any kind.

Their mom cleared her throat as she shuffled food around on her plate. That's all she would ever do, shuffle the food. Actually eating it was asking too much of her. She'd eat a few of the vegetables to soothe the burning ache of hunger in her gut, but that would be it until morning when she'd drink a kale smoothie and call it good until dinner. "Beth, honey, tell us what happened with you today. Anything exciting?"

Beth broke the staring match. "Nothing much. Mrs. Williams is back on her medicine. I saw her sneak one of the tiny pink pills after lunch. A few students are planning a party this weekend because their parents are out of town. Silvia wants me to go with her, but I'm not sure about it."

"I think it would be a wonderful idea." Yeah, leave it to their mother to encourage them, their seventeen- and fifteen-year-old daughters, to go party hard. "It may be the fun you need."

Beth and Nora's eyes met again, and they couldn't help but giggle. Their parents were so predictable. Their dad the driving force for academic excellence while their mother focused more on the social aspect of it all. The girls knew how to play them both and knew the reactions they would get. Nora wouldn't be surprised if Beth hadn't made up the party bit just to get a rise out of their mother.

"How was debate today?" Dad asked. Nora froze. How did he know about debate? He only ever asked when there was a competition. When Nora didn't answer him right away, he looked up to find her staring at him. It made him uncomfortable and he cleared his throat. "I saw Danny today, Brittany's dad. He stopped by the office to get some financial advice. He mentioned it."

Nora's heart rate picked up again. She could always lie and say it was great and leave it at that. But she'd never lied to her parents before. She'd never had a reason. Things were different now. She had a secret and she wanted to keep it. If they were to ever find out, she was sure they would put her in counseling or ship her off to a boarding school where her every move was accounted for. She had to lie to keep whatever freedom she had.

"It was fine," her voice cracked, and she cleared her throat. *I wonder who I get that habit from?* She almost laughed at her own sarcasm, but she held it in check. She didn't want to have to explain herself in the midst of an 'it was fine' lie.

They finished dinner with a little more conversation. Nora went back up to her room after being excused. She'd no sooner got settled into her chair with a book when Beth came barging into her room.

"I didn't think you had it in you. You liar."

Nora blushed, hating that someone had caught onto her lie. She should have known Beth would catch it. She was observant like that. A little flush of anger followed as her words truly sank in. That was the second time that day she'd been told someone didn't think she had it in her. People would probably be surprised at what was in her thoughts sometimes.

"I'm not a total prude, Beth. Besides, it wasn't like I lied about something major. So I skipped a meeting? It's not that big of a deal."

Beth plopped down on the bed, her eyes wide with disbelief. "Not that big of a deal? Nora, I can count the number of times you lied to Mom and Dad on one hand. Plus, let's not mention that you are the vice president of the debate team and you missing a meeting for any other reason besides death is kind of a big deal, which is why you lied."

Nora tossed her book aside and laid her head back against the chair so she was starring up at the ceiling. This was stupid. She shouldn't have to worry about one stupid little lie like this, nor should she have to justify her actions to her sister.

"How are you feeling today?" It was petty, she knew that, but turning the attention on Beth always worked. Beth always lost focus when it came to talking about herself or when she was put on the spot.

She looked down at her feet while her toes followed the pattern on the rug. "I can't shake the thoughts," she whispered. "It's like an infection that just won't go away. I keep trying everything my therapist says to do, with hope that it will work, but it never does."

Now Nora felt guilty. She should have never used her sister's weakness to get away from her own problems. Standing, she went over and sat by Beth. "What is it this time?" It wasn't meant to sound rude or disrespectful. Beth's mind switched tactics on her regularly. It seemed like every few weeks the thoughts would change. They'd root in her brain and fester for a few weeks, then in would come a new seed ready to take root.

Beth seemed to shrivel in on herself. Her bony shoulder blades stuck up to hide her face. "I keep getting paranoid about my friends. Are they being real with me? Do they even care if I'm there? I'm sure they say things behind my back." She shakes her head causing a tear to escape. "It keeps me up at night."

"It's gotten that bad?" Nora had suspected when she saw her sister at dinner, but she was hoping she was wrong. Beth losing sleep only made things worse.

"Yeah." Tears beamed in Beth's eyes as their eyes met. "I don't know how to stop them," she whispered.

Nora held onto her sister tight. "We will do it together. You hear me? Anytime, I don't care what time it is, you come to me. Don't let this rob you into thinking you have no one because you always have me." Nora always did her best when it came to her sister, but often-times like Beth, she'd lay awake worried she wasn't doing enough.

They spent the rest of the evening curled up on Nora's bed binge watching shows on Netflix. When Beth started to go to her room, Nora stopped her. She didn't want her sister to be alone, not tonight. She wasn't always going to be there for her sister, not with college coming up in a year, but she wanted to do what she could while she was here. Beth needed her, needed their strong bond, if for nothing else than to get a sound night of sleep.

They'd just settled under the covers, the giant king-sized bed more than enough for the two of them as was the down comforter her mother had made to fit their beds perfectly, when her phone vibrated on the nightstand.

Liv: Have you heard?

Beth leaned over to see the screen. "Liv? Who's that? I don't know anyone who goes to our school named Liv."

Nora panicked for a nanosecond. Though she trusted and loved Beth, she didn't want her knowing about this. "She doesn't."

Beth tried to ask more questions, but Nora shut her out by rolling over.

Nora: Heard what?

Liv: They found a body in the lake about an hour ago.

Nora's stomach dropped. A body in the lake? She thought back to her index cards she had at the library. It had to be a coincidence.

Nora: Was it an accident?

Her heart pounded as she watched the three little bubbles dance across her screen, indicating Liv was typing.

Liv: I'm not sure. They haven't released much detail about it.

Nora couldn't go off hearsay. She needed to know the facts and know them now. Was it a murder? An accident? Things like this didn't happen in their small town. Robberies and fist fights, sure. Murders, no. It was killing her not knowing the facts. Liv said she'd get back to her as soon as she heard more.

Nora clicked off her messages and opened Instagram. It was time to do some stalking. An hour later, as she waited for her newsfeed to refresh once again with no news, Liv texted her again.

Liv: They just released the name.

Nora: Where are you getting your information? I can't find anything and I'm refreshing now.

Liv: My uncle is a cop. I live with him and my aunt.

That took Nora by surprise. How had she never known that. *Oh, right, because you're the queen of no small talk.*

Liv: I'll explain later. Right now, you need to hear this.

Nora's heart started racing again. Her gut tightened to the point she thought she was going to be sick. This was not going to be good.

Liv: Seventeen-year-old male, Kyle Austin, was found with multiple lacerations to his face and body. Cause of death, tbd, though preliminaries believe it to be blunt force trauma.

Her hands shook as she read the message and she sank to the floor, unable to hold herself up anymore. *It couldn't be. It couldn't.* She began reassuring herself that Liv was playing some sort of sick joke on her when her phone buzzed again. This time is was a notification from Snapchat. It was Liv. Nora's stomach twisted as she clicked on the yellow app arranged in the center of her screen.

It was a picture of Liv, sitting in a cop car with a walkie talkie in hand. Caption at the bottom reads *"I'd make a great spy."*

She probably wasn't even supposed to be with her uncle. Liv was good about getting into things she had no business poking around. She'd done it multiple times at her school, or so Charlie had told her.

Nora hit the reply button but then froze. What was she supposed to say? *Oh cool, isn't that a fun coincidence.* It wasn't a joke. It also wasn't something Nora could casually talk about over a snap. If Liv was being for real and this wasn't some lame joke, this could all come back on her.

But how?

Her stomach clenched with fear and this time she had no choice. She threw up.

Chapter Three

It was all over the news. Every channel was blasting Kyle's picture along with the news of his body being discovered in the lake. Nora's mom sat at the bar, coffee mug in hand, clothes freshly pressed and neatly arranged on her body. She was staring with worry at the television.

"This is terrible," she said without taking her eyes off the television.

Nora poured herself a cup of coffee. "It is," she agreed, not knowing what else to say. Not only was the shock of what happened still seeping into her mind, but the lack of sleep was also playing with her. She'd tossed and turned all night, thinking about what had happened and how close it aligned to her murder scene for the club that same night.

How could anyone have known? She'd changed her mind at the last moment.

Was it a coincidence? If so, it was a mighty big one considering Kyle had died the exact same way she'd portrayed in her notes.

Were Liv and Charlie involved in some way? That was a possibility she didn't want to think about. She'd trusted them. They trusted her. She couldn't start doubting them now at the drop of a hat.

"Are you okay?" Nora jostled and found her mother was now standing at the counter directly across from her. Concern pinched at her eyebrows and she was worrying her lip with her teeth. Her mother was prone to overreacting to everything. It wouldn't surprise her if she came home from school to find her mother had organized a dinner of some kind for the parents and kids affected by the tragedy, because lobster bisque and salad was a cure all for trauma, right?

"I'm fine," she answered and took another sip of her coffee. A simple answer like that wasn't going to suffice. She needed to give her mother more. "I'm a little worried about how dramatic school is going to be today. I didn't know Kyle that well, but it sucks. Today's just going to be long and awkward." *Now, you're oversharing. Stop it.*

"Awkward? Nora, there's nothing awkward about death if you don't look at it selfishly. It's a tragedy. It's sad." The disappointment she was accustomed to receiving from her mother shone bright. "Quit thinking of yourself, Nora."

Anger burned through her, making her hotter than the coffee ever could. *How dare she accuse me of being selfish.* "I learn it from the best," Nora snarled. She left the room with her mom watching her retreat, shock heavy on her face. She didn't know if it was from the lack of sleep or the stress of what happened, but she never talked back to her mother like that. She'd wanted to, came close a few times, but had never actually gone through with it. Beth was usually that role taker.

The morning air was crisp and cool. The ground glistened, as if it was coated with a dusting of diamonds. Once the sun got high enough, the diamonds would melt and the dead grass would reveal its ugly self once again.

Nora pulled her jacket closer to her. *Only three more weeks until spring.* She tried pepping herself up, but it was a lie. Winter would linger well into the spring. It always did. She couldn't wait until she was eighteen, had multiple scholarships in hand, and was moving further south. She couldn't wait to get away from this miserable place.

"Hey!"

A scream burst out of Nora, as if she was being kidnapped and it was her last farewell to the earth. Laughter tore through her terror and Liv and Charlie came from out behind the bushes.

"You're a jumpy one this morning," Liv said, sauntering up the sidewalk, a smile still broad on her face. Charlie was still laughing at her side.

Panicked at seeing them there, in her yard, she rushed toward them and pulled them off to the side away from the windows. Her mom was still inside and if she caught a glimpse of the two it would all be over. She would want to know who they were and then demand to know why Nora was hanging around them. It was pathetic, really. To have to hide her friends and true interests all for the sake of not hearing a lecture at the end of the day or be questioned as to why she was wasting her time with people who didn't have the same drive as she did. Her parents wouldn't see her friends as just that, friends. No, they would see Liv and Charlie as two girls threatening to lead their daughter away from the sheltered, elite life they had built for her.

"What are you doing here?" she hissed, then winced once she heard the tone she was carrying. If Liv and

Charlie turned around and left without another word to her ever again, she would understand. She would probably do the same.

As expected, Charlie narrowed her eyes at the question. She was the defensive one of the two. She had to be. According to her, her family was always being blamed and questioned for the scandalous things going on around her neighborhood because of the tattoos her dad sported from decades of bad decisions. Decisions he was trying to leave behind and start a new life for his family.

"We came to see if you were okay," Liv said, a little snappy.

Guilt spread through Nora. *Quit being like your parents.* As much as she hated to remind herself of it, that's exactly how she was acting. Ashamed and threatened by the sight of her friends standing in her yard. She'd never felt more pathetic in her life than she did in that moment.

She took a deep breath. "I'm sorry." Tears stung at the back of her eyes, but she pushed them away. "I'm being shitty, but I don't mean to be. My mom, she's just... protective." It was the best reasoning she could give without coming out calling it as it was, prejudice at its finest.

"Don't blame your mother for the choices you make. That's all on you." Charlie was right. Hearing her and making a choice of her own, Nora looped her arms through the girls' arms and led them to the front walk and toward the sidewalk. She didn't care if her mama saw them. She didn't care if her neighbors saw them. She wasn't going to become the type of person she despised. She'd taken enough ass chewings in the past, what was one more when it meant she could be real?

"I hope you know this doesn't completely ease the burn you just dished out," Charlie said.

"I do," Nora replied, "but I hope it soothes it." She fluttered her eyes and gave her best smile. "Besides, I'm going to need you guys to keep me sane the next few days. I barely slept a wink last night."

"Is that why you look like shit?" Liv nudged her in the side.

"Another part is this god-awful outfit." Charlie tugged on Nora's blazer, the one with the plaid arm cuffs and golden crested symbol on the breast pocket. It was bland next to Charlie's loose-fitting black sweater, colorful leggings, and bright red coat. "I would not be caught dead in this thing."

"I don't know," Liv chimed in, "It kind of gives off a Harry Potter feel." She winked at Nora. "Feeling magical?"

She chuckled. "I wish."

"Nora, wait up!"

They stopped and turned to find Beth running to catch up with them. Just before she reached them, Beth stopped and looked from Liv to Charlie. Nora could only imagine what was going through her mind.

"Are these your friends or should I run the other way while dialing 911?" Beth asked, while staring at Liv. Before Nora could answer, she continued, "Because honestly, I didn't think you had it in you to have friends this cool."

Ouch. "Very funny, Beth." Nora gave a quick introduction, then turned on her sister. "I thought you were staying home today to... ya know... rest." Beth sleeping in her room last night had been comforting in a way, but also exhausting. She hadn't been able to fall asleep but couldn't really do anything to remedy the problem out of fear of waking Beth. She knew her sister needed all the sleep she could get, considering her thoughts and nightmares kept her up most of the time.

"I was, until I found out Mom was staying home today. No, thank you." Given her mother's extreme tendencies to hover and Beth's need for space, yeah, that probably wasn't a good idea. "Besides, the harder I push myself the better."

A honk split through the morning air as a car pulled up to the curb. Nora's heart skipped a beat as she turned to find Mrs. Bright, aka Mrs. Nosey Noose, waving with a big, fake smile plastered on her face. Mrs. Bright lived down the street, kept the phones hot, and would toast anyone she heard a good gossip piece about. She didn't care if it totally ruined them or not, as long as she was getting the attention and spreading the word she didn't care. Her daughter was worse. Nora eyed Kenzie in the front seat.

Just what I need right now. "Hi, Mrs. Bright," Nora said, her own fake smile in place.

"Ass kisser," Beth whispered in her ear. Sadly, she wasn't wrong. Nora kept herself in check, even when she wanted to be a bitch.

"Hello, girls. Kenzie's car wouldn't start this morning and I'm having to give her a lift to school. Would you two like a ride?" Heat pulsed through Nora. She wasn't even acknowledging Liv and Charlie, who were standing right there with her and Beth. Mrs. Bright didn't know them, so therefore they were automatically irrelevant.

"Thanks, but we're catching up with friends. We're okay walking." Beth elbowed her in the side, but she ignored it. Normally, the girls got to school by their father's driver, but he had taken their father to the airport that morning and hadn't made it back in time. Nora still hadn't gotten her license so that left her only one option, walk. At the moment, that was a much better choice than riding with those two. "Thanks for the consideration, though."

Mrs. Bright resigned herself to the decline. "Tell your mother we said hello." With a wave, she pulled away from the curb and headed toward Northeast Pinewood.

"Are you insane?" Beth asked. "It's freezing, and that was a free ride!"

"Then why didn't you go?" Nora challenged, although she knew why. Her sister wouldn't be able to handle the stress of going with Mrs. Bright without Nora by her side. Her anxiety would eat her alive and she'd be bothered the rest of the day.

"You know that woman gives me the creeps," Beth mumbled.

Nora laced her arm through Beth's. "That's because she is a creep."

"I don't know that I will ever get used to you elite, rich people," Charlie mused as they continued down the walk. "You're all so fake, cunning, and yet, painfully aware of each other's insecurities. It seems too intrusive and hard. I don't want to be anything but real."

Nora envied her for that. If she was to ever tell her parents about half the things she truly enjoyed, they'd tell her she was being silly and wasting her time. Everything done needed to have a purpose, a true purpose. Joy was not a true purpose, not in the least.

Beth chattered on with Charlie about the ins and outs of public school. She was fascinated with the simplicity of it. That was until Liv chimed in and told her about all the drugs and police officers that patrolled the lots frequently. That shut Beth down really quick. She was terrified of anything that sounded dangerous. That brought Nora back to Kyle and the similarities between his death and her game at the meeting yesterday. Was it just a coincidence?

Once they reached the gates that encased Northeast Pinewood Academy, Nora urged Beth to run along. Being late set Beth on edge, plus she needed a moment alone with Liv and Charlie.

"Do you guys think I have anything to worry about?" Nora asked once Beth was out of earshot.

Charlie shrugged, giving her no real signs as to what she thought about the situation. As usual, it was Liv who took the stage. Liv was the more reasonable of the two, while Charlie was the backbone and took crap from no one. "I don't think so." She looked to Charlie and bit her lip. There was an unspoken question between the two of them, but it was going to be up to Liv to ask it. Charlie looked away, seeming distracted and unwilling to participate in whatever was about to happen. Liv sighed. "Well, I mean, that is if you didn't do it. You didn't, did you?"

Shock with a punch of anger hit Nora hard. *Is she being for real right now?* By the look on Liv's concerned face, she knew she was. "I can't believe you are even asking me that. Are you insane? We played these stupid games to sharpen our senses, not to get off on some weird ass dream to carry them through." At least she hadn't. She had one goal in mind, and that was to become an FBI profiler. What about Liv and Charlie, though? "At least, *I* didn't."

That snapped Charlie's attention back to the conversation. "What's that supposed to mean?"

What was that supposed to mean? Were they really here discussing it? Blaming each other? Up until six months ago, Nora thought she was the only freak in town who was obsessed with the news and dissecting every murder in the state before it could be solved. She'd take the facts given to the public and then run with it. Who does that? Crazy people! That's what she used to tell herself anyway. She'd been so relieved to discover she wasn't alone. Was she really going to throw it all away because of one incident, even if that incident was murder?

Nora took a deep breath and tried centering herself. She didn't want to say anything else that would add to this fire. "I didn't mean anything by it, no more than Liv did when she asked me." They both looked between each other, guilty, but also a little ticked. "Okay, look," she tried again, seeing as how this wasn't going anywhere good. "It's been a scary night, but I don't think we have anything to worry about. Do you two? I mean, we're all innocent." She didn't like the edge of doubt that frizzled in her stomach.

"You're right," Liv said. "It's just so weird, ya know?"

"Yeah, tell me about," Nora huffed. The three agreed to lay low before parting ways with promises of keeping in touch.

Turning toward the front gates, Nora took a deep breath and braced herself. As expected, it was a mad house full of whispers and fake tears. Teachers discussed the murder in low tones as they stood outside their classrooms. Girls stood in front of their lockers crying, as if they really cared about Kyle. No one cared about Kyle; that was a common fact. He was arrogant. He was a jerk because he could be. He was the bad kid of the school everyone steered clear of him in fear of what accusations would be made about them. Because everyone knew, if you wanted something done but didn't want to do it yourself, Kyle would do it for you. For a hefty payment no less. Being associated with him only meant you got your name attached to the rep.

Nora kept her face blank. She wasn't sad over Kyle's death, although it was a terrible tragedy. Guilt was weighing heavy on her. Why didn't she feel the need to bawl her eyes out like the other attention seekers lining the halls? She knew she should feel some sort of sympathy for what happened. He was a classmate, a kid the same age as her, and who had gone there since the sixth grade. Yet, no matter how much she kept telling herself this, she couldn't bring herself to feel anything for Kyle. Did that make her as guilty as the murderer? Or as psychotic?

Not wanting to be judged for not crying her eyes out like all the other preps in the hall who acted as if Kyle was at their house every Friday night hanging out and eating popcorn – even though that was a total joke – she plastered on a frown and kept her head low. When she reached her locker, she grabbed her morning books and was ready to disappear into homeroom when she knocked into the wall of doors and locks.

Glancing over her shoulder as she righted herself, she saw Reed Benson standing there looking at her. His eyes were wild, his hair wild, his clothes wild from not being properly ironed and tucked. Everything about him screamed wild. That's how Nora had always thought of Reed, as wild.

"I'm sorry," he said, his voice deep and his gaze looking at her but seeming unfocused. "I'm a little out of it this morning."

Heat exploded through her. Not only did she not know what to say to him, considering he had just lost his best friend, but she'd never heard him utter a word since his move here. Kyle had always done the talking.

"It's fine," she said, adjusting the strap of her backpack. "How are you holding up?" she asked, figuring no one else would bother checking on him. They were too worried about their own fake feelings. Reed was the one who had really lost a friend.

Reed shrugged and shoved his hands deeper into his pockets. "It's weird, you know? Going to bed thinking how it should be, even if it's not where you want it to be, and then waking up to find some of the should be is gone."

Nora's face fell. That had been deep and something she didn't know how to respond to other than a typical 'I know what you mean' statement that lacked empathy.

Reed must have taken her fallen face and lack of response the wrong way as he shrugged again and said, "I'm good, though, holding up."

"That's good," she said, knowing she needed to say something this time. "Let me know if you need anything." It was her standard line. No one ever came knocking and asking for help, which was why she mostly stuck to it. It was polite and the right thing to say, but she knew no one would ever follow up. She would later find out she was wrong.

Relief did not come in her homeroom English class like it usually did. The teacher droned on and on about Kyle's death, the grief counselor's availability at the office, the principal's fears of student moral, again with the grief counselor, and then she wrapped it up with a speech on bullying. Nora wasn't really sure where the bullying part fit in to the murder. Suicide had been ruled out and announced this morning.

It wasn't until the intercom chimed with an announcement during her third period science class that Nora snapped to attention.

Attention students and faculty, as many of you know we recently lost one of our own, Kyle Austin. He was found in the lake late last night. The conditions of his death are unknown at this time, however, we would like to extend our condolences to his family, friends, and the student body. We will be holding a memorial service for Mr. Austin on Monday, April 21ˢᵗ at 6:00 in the school's chapel. We encourage all students to attend as your way of bringing closure and support to our community over this tragic event.

"It's terrible isn't it?" Nora jumped at the sudden hot breath on her cheek and looked over her shoulder at Gary, the captain of the debate team, as he leaned over his desk a bit too close for her comfort. "Who do you think did it?"

Nora flinched, wondering why he would ask her that, but then stopped the train wreck happening in her head. He didn't know about the group. This was Gary, a guy who liked a good debate and was always looking for an opening to do so. Who killed Kyle was nothing but a debate to him.

"How am I supposed to know?" she said, then winced at the offensive tone she had. "I mean, I didn't know him that well. It would be hard for me to judge."

"True," he drawled, "but I'm banking on some street gang. Think about it, drowned in the lake with lacerations. This screams payment murder."

The look on her face said it all. He was an idiot. "This isn't New York City, genius. It's Lake Placid. There hasn't been a murder here since Old Man Gene lost his crap and killed his wife five years ago." Even though she'd only been twelve, she still remembered the uproar from the event. Old Man Gene had created quite the stir in their small town. People still shuddered when they talked about it.

A glint filled Gary's eyes that Nora didn't like. "Kyle could be the first of many more to come."

Choosing not to indulge him on his wild fantasies, she turned back around and started working on her daily notes sheet before the lesson began. Every day Mrs. Wilmer put notes on the board for students to copy. They had five minutes and then she'd kill the projector and off they went into the lesson. One thing Mrs. Wilmer had done was improve Nora's hand writing skills, but she didn't know jack about science.

Chapter Four

By the time she got home that night, her nerves were shot. All day long she had heard nothing but speculations as to what really happened to Kyle. Some claimed he had been murdered by his parents, others thought he was dealt with by a gang notorious in town (though the worst they had ever done was rip off a bell ringer over Christmas break), while the rest claimed he did it himself even though suicide was already ruled out. Nora didn't believe any of those things, but the speculation was driving her mad.

Excusing herself from dinner with a murmured excuse of not feeling well, she headed up to her room to make a list. Beth eyed her as she went, but she ignored her sister's judgmental eyes. She would question her later, no doubt, and that's when Nora would deal with it. Beth was no idiot. Whatever Nora came up with as a cover would have to be believable.

Changing into her favorite soft pajamas with paint stains splattered on the legs, she grabbed a notebook and got comfortable in the gray, overstuffed chair tucked in the corner. It had been a gift from Beth, as were the pants. Her mom hated the chair, especially since it came from an estate auction. It didn't matter that the house was right down the street and ten times nicer than their house. Her mom had considered it tacky and demanded they get rid of it. What she didn't account for was being ganged up on by her two daughters, ultimately losing the battle.

The accusations of the day ran through her mind, as did the speculations from the news. Nora thought once she got home from school she'd be able to get away from it all for a little while. She'd been wrong. It was all she could think about. She had this deep fear it would come back to haunt her somehow. Liv and Charlie told her not to worry about it, but it's what she did when she felt overwhelmed by something. Beth was the same way, but Nora was able to handle the worry better than Beth.

Rolling her shoulders and taking a deep breath, she thought about the debate coming up tomorrow. She had to focus on that. Northeast was undefeated and she wanted to keep it that way. It was her senior year and being vice president of an undefeated team would do wonders for her transcript.

Nora: Have you started your frontlines?

She texted Gary then started reading over her highlights. She'd gone through all the reading for possible evidence that could be presented in the debate. As always, she highlighted possible arguments that could arise and made frontlines to research. She'd meant to have the last two done last night, but when news of Kyle broke, so did her concentration.

Her phoned chimed and she read Gary's response.

Gary: Are you kidding me? Are you just now doing your frontlines? Our tournament starts at 8:00 AM!

She rolled her eyes. She knew what time the tournament started. She was also very well aware of how important this match was. The last thing she needed was for Gary to get his ego in a tighter knot.

Nora: I'm finished with my Frontlines.

It was a fib, but only by two short questions he didn't even know she'd written. The frontlines were their choice to choose and research. There was evidence in the past she'd only written two frontlines for because she knew the material inside and out. The number of frontlines depended on the debater and their knowledge of the topics that could be talked about.

Nora: Was checking to see if you were done and wanted to compare notes.

His reply was instant.

Gary: We practiced Frontlines yesterday. You know, the meeting you missed.

Aggravated, she tossed her phone aside. There was no need to deal with his attitude when she had enough to worry about. She'd practiced a hundred times by herself before, she didn't mind doing it again. What was the big deal of one missed practice anyway? It was one practice, not the whole season.

Gary didn't bother texting her anything else. Nora didn't figure he would. She lost herself in her research of science and the effects it had on the earth. She stood strong when it came to this topic, knowing all benefits science provided not only for humans but the earth itself. The questions came when the negative side of the conversation arose. She'd believed in science her whole life and had never questioned its negative sides before. Yes, they were there, but so were the benefits.

She lost herself in the research, not giving one thought to Kyle. Okay, correction, she thought about him one time when the mention of DNA testing had come across the research paper she'd been reading. Her mind spaced while she wondered if they'd found DNA evidence on him, and if so, when they'd release that information to the public. A little peace of mind would be nice.

As she was reading her negative arguments out loud about chemical pollutants in the ground, Beth flung herself through the door, slammed it, and flopped down on the bed belly first.

"I hate my life," she mumbled into the navy blue and purple comforter.

Nora let her pencil fall from her lap. This conversation wasn't going to be over in thirty seconds so she could proceed with her argument. Nope. Beth was in a deep sea of bad mood and it was going to take hours of positive affirmations to pull her back to shore. She shook off the irritation. Her sister needed her, and according to the therapist, she could feel when they were being fake or annoyed. Nora didn't want to contribute to that. So, as always, she dug down deep in her soul and found the sadness she kept there for Beth, along with the love. "You have no reason to hate your life. You're amazing and we love you."

She rolled over onto her back and stared at the ceiling. "Are you sure about that? Because I think Mom and Dad are tired of me." Before Nora could tell her some line about their parents not being tired of her, they were just worried like everyone else, her sister pushed ahead. "I can't believe you left me at dinner like that. I thought we had a pact?"

They did? "I must be unaware of this so-called pact." Nora thought back to all the pacts she'd ever made with Beth: Don't leave me in the mall alone, people are weird. Birthdays were made for pancakes and whipped cream served in bed, never forget. If you can tell I'm lying, cover me and I'll explain later. Not once did the two of them make a pact to live through the torture of dinner for one another.

Beth sighed. "It's unspoken, Nora. Sister code is to never leave one another in an awkward situation if it can be avoided."

She wasn't sure what sister handbook of crap she was reading, but she was going to have to find it and burn it. "Look, I really didn't feel well and I needed to come up here to study." She'd planned on giving this big spill with a good punch line to make Beth believe her, but it didn't happen. She'd gotten sidetracked with trying to occupy her own mind away from life, lies, and worries.

"Since when do you need to study for a tournament. You're essentially Google with legs and boobs." Beth rolled over onto her side and propped up her head with her hand. She glared at Nora. "What's really going on?"

Her heart went wild as heat rolled through her body. She needed to lie, but she didn't know how to lie to Beth. Beth was the one person who could look at Nora and read her like a book. They were close, always had been. Beth knew every move Nora made meant something: an eye twitch, biting her lip, cracking her knuckles, drumming her fingers on her leg, everything.

She had no choice but to try and get away with a semi-truth. "You heard about one of my classmates dying, right?" She was sure she had, but sometimes Beth could get stuck in her own head. It was why the doctor had suggested she start journaling. She could lay out her problems in clear script while focusing on one thing at a time.

"You mean the one Mom was crying about over dinner? Yeah, I heard."

Cathy, always the dramatic one. "What was she saying?"

Beth waved her free hand in the air and then let it fall onto the mattress. "Oh, you know Mom. She's worried about you, the neighbor's kids, probably their dogs' kids too. We may have to have a community dinner to mourn this loss together."

Nora groaned. She'd known from the look in her mother's eyes that morning that she'd want to make some spectacle out of Kyle's death, even though she didn't know the kid. "Of course, she does." She let the aggravation that was starting to build because of her mother slide off her like butter. Nora didn't have room for nor did she care how her mother acted anymore. It was no surprise to them. "You know me. I'm not one for attention, and I think that's because I've always been embarrassed of Mom's elaborate schemes to get it herself, but I can't shake his death. It being all anyone talked about today didn't help, which is why I needed to step out and take a breather."

"And study? I could think of a lot of better ways to take a breather." Beth flopped back on the bed with a dramatic sigh. Though they both didn't want to be like their mother, if there was one who was going to be just like her, it was Beth. Nora was more like their father, reserved yet dramatic in the privacy of his own space.

Nora's phone buzzed. Glancing down at the screen, she saw it was Liv.

Liv: My uncle will kill me if this gets out, so you have to secret phone swear not to say anything. If you do, I will gut you.

The threat screamed out at Nora. She wasn't one to handle confrontations well. The person who always backed down and gave into the fight, yeah, that was her.

Nora: Who am I going to tell?

It wasn't like she had any friends at Northeast. They all thought of her as the spoiled rich girl who thought she was smarter than everyone else. The fact of the matter was, she wasn't any of those things. She wasn't rich, her parents were. She had to account for every dollar she spent to her dad, who had been the one to bring himself from nothing to a man well known around town. She heard the stories and got the post card, several times. She also didn't see herself as the smartest. She struggled just like everyone else. Math was a nightmare that she had to work twice as hard at just to get a low average A. She didn't talk to anyone, well, because she didn't like anyone.

Liv: Your sister.

Nora stared at her phone, apprehension tearing through her. She had confided in Liv and Charlie during one of their meetings that Beth was the only true friend she had. They hadn't believed her at first. Why would they? She was rich. She went to private school. She had it all. That's what it looked like on the outside, how could it not be the same on the inside? Just like a present can look beautiful on the outside and hold the worst gift in the world inside, life at Northeast was the same. Beautiful on the outside, ugly on the inside. You just had to stop and recognize it.

Nora: I won't tell her. I can't.

As much as she would love to tell her sister about everything happening, she couldn't. It would torment Beth and cause her anxiety to be worse than it was on normal days, which wasn't all that great. The only people she had to ease her mind with all of this were Liv and Charlie.

Nora watched as the three bubbles danced across her screen and waited for Liv's reply. When the message appeared, she held her breath as she read it.

Liv: Don't make me regret this. Tox report came back with traces of chloroform.

Nora gasped as she stared down at the screen. Speculations started forming in her head. Was it someone she trusted? Nora couldn't see thugs who knock off Christmas bell ringers wasting their time on chloroform. Aren't gangs supposed to gut and dump? Next, she had to wonder if the person had been too small and weak to overpower him.

Next thing she knew, her mind was going where she didn't want it to go. Had the person purposefully used chloroform to make it seem like it was someone who couldn't overpower Kyle, someone like her. Suddenly, she couldn't breathe and her heart was pounding so hard she was sure it would explode, which was a real possibility although some people didn't believe that. A cardiac rupture happens when the –

"Nora!"

She jerked and looked up at Beth, eyes wide.

"What in the hell is wrong with you?" Before she could answer, Beth narrowed her eyes and held out her hand. "Don't give me any crap about spacing out on info processing or some crap. You freaked out and got lost in here," she pointed to her head. "Trust me, I know the look and the feeling."

She wasn't sure how much longer she could keep this secret. The weight of the lies was already starting to add up. "Gary texted me. He's being an ass because I missed that meeting yesterday. It's not like I don't know what I'm doing, but he's acting like I skip out on them all the time. You know how I get when people are upset with me." Two truths and a semi-lie, she'd take it. Gary was obviously upset with her. He'd never denied her an opportunity to study together if it meant it strengthened their chances of winning. She'd always wondered what his home life was like but had never bothered asking. That opened a door to him asking the same and that was one topic she didn't want to discuss with anyone. Another truth, she did hate when people got upset with her. It was a terrible curse she wished she could break, but so far, no luck. If someone looked at her crossed eyed, she would analyze it for days. The lie was that she didn't give a crap about Gary being upset with her. He could be upset with her all he wanted. Right now, she had to focus on what was happening real time, like the possibility of someone trying to frame her for murder.

Liv: Radio silence, meaning, you're freaking out. Stop! It doesn't mean anything.

Nora smiled down at the phone. Her friends were getting to know her so well.

"Screw Gary and all those debate naysayers. They can kiss your ass." But nobody had her back like Beth.

~

Nora was reading over her highlights while Gary went to determine if the team was pro or con for the tournament. The others waited patiently at the side of the stage. This was the part Nora hated. Gary would come back, tell the team where they stood in the debate, have a sheet of topics that would be addressed, and then choose the debaters he thought best suited the topics for each round. Sometimes, everyone played a part. Sometimes, they didn't. She hated witnessing the disappointment on the faces of those who wouldn't be participating.

She hated confrontation outside the debate ring. It was why she hadn't pushed to become president. She didn't want to be vice president either, but Gary was all about winning, and with Nora's outstanding record for delivering her arguments in the allotted time, filling the clock, and having no hesitation when asked a question, she knew he would select her. No one else had been surprised either, although Stacey had tried arguing against her position. Stacey had her eye on the debate team before Nora gave it a thought. She could remember back in middle school when Stacey often talked about joining the elite team. Seventh and eighth grade was the only chance given to prove you belonged on the senior high debate team. Fail the junior team, there was no way you were getting on the senior team. When sixth grade started coming to an end, Stacey would check the website three to four times a day for the signup sheet to become available while also driving Nora up the wall wanting to know if she'd heard anything. The day those signups went live was one of the best days of Nora's sixth grade year.

"Hello, Nora."

Startled, she turned to find Stacey's mom smiling at her with her twenty-thousand-dollar smile, at least that's what Nora had heard. "Oh, hello, Mrs. Hollis. How are you?"

"Wonderful, thank you." She turned toward the stage and gestured to the others. "Glad to see the whole team is here today."

Nora tensed. Without a doubt in her mind, she knew that was a jab at her. No one on the team had ever missed a tournament. Besides her, only one other member had missed a practice and that was due to the flu… a year ago. Stacey no doubt went home blabbing to her mother. They had both been gunning for Stacey to earn a higher spot on the team. She was sure they were watching her every move.

"Yeah, me too," she replied, trying her best to keep her frustration out of her tone.

"Gary should be out here any minute to tell us our standings and who will be discussing which topics."

Mrs. Hollis's lips tightened. "Well, let's hope he doesn't put in that dreadful Brittany." *Oh yeah, the girls have definitely been gossiping.*

Again, she was glad she wasn't president. "I'm sure he will make the best decisions."

Mrs. Hollis made small talk with Nora before walking over to Stacey and giving her one final pep talk, or so her and Beth liked to call it, one final pep-or-you're-going-to-get-it talks.

The debate went as it always did, with the students pumped and ready for more while parents fell asleep in the back. Well, not all the parents. The prestigious parents, the ones whose lives depended on whether their kid got five minutes of argument time or thirty.

Nora was walking out, hoping her parents remembered what time she said to pick her up. Debates were not their cup of tea, as her mother had so politely put it, not even when it was hosted five miles from their house. Her father was honest with her and said he had more pressing matters to attend than listening to teenagers argue over things they did not understand. Last time she'd gotten embarrassed and almost took the bus after waiting for over an hour for them to show up. Turned out, it was Nora's fault for not texting them a reminder. She'd been sure to do that today.

An uneasy feeling settled over her as she walked out to the parking lot. It felt as if someone was watching her. She'd tried not looking obvious as she glanced around the area and over tops of cars. When her phone rang, she about jumped out of her skin.

Flipping the phone over, she saw it was Charlie. "You scared the crap out of me," she answered in way of greeting.

"My question is, why are you so jumpy?" The amusement was clear in her voice.

Nora tried hunching in between her shoulders to shield herself. "I feel like I'm being watched."

"So, you're being paranoid." Something rustled in the background and Charlie hissed at someone to go away. Before Nora could ask her who it was, she was talking again. "You shouldn't be paranoid. I've seen killers, Nora. You're no killer."

That was comforting. "I can't help it." It was the truth. She really couldn't. "I find it odd, and when I find something odd, I have to figure it out."

"Don't go figuring this one out," Charlie instructed, her voice sharp. "You start poking around, you'll end up framing yourself or something. Let the pros handle this one. Your time to shine as a detective will come soon enough!"

Nora didn't bother correcting her. The fact Charlie was in the same career bubble Nora was planning for the future thrilled her. She thought the only other person on the planet who listened and remembered was Beth. "Not that I'm not happy to hear from you, but is everything okay? You've never called me before." She'd given both girls her number after their second meeting, but Charlie had never used it until now.

Charlie chuckled. "It is a little odd for me to be calling, huh? I'm not much of a phone person. I'll cut to the chase. I was scrolling through Instagram and saw someone posted the memorial is on Monday. Are you going?"

The thought of the memorial made her queasy. "I'm not sure yet. Why?"

"I think you should go. Liv thinks otherwise." That would be the reason for the call then. Nora hated when those two didn't see eye to eye. They would argue and both want to be heard. The confrontations always made Nora feel uncomfortable. Liv would be calling her in no time. "I think it would be good for you to be seen, you know, in case something did come up in the future. Which I totally don't think is going to happen," she added in a rush.

It was a valid point, and a scary one. Nora had done her research. Cops often scoped out memorials to profile the mourners. Who was there to mourn and who was there to revel in their handiwork? "I'll think about it."

A car horn blared and a mom waved frantically at one of the girls waiting outside. The girl, surprised, rushed over and got into the car. "Where are you?" Charlie asked.

"Oh, I had a debate tournament today," Nora answered. "I'm waiting on my mom to pick me up."

"Girl, why didn't you tell us? We would have come to cheer you on." Charlie sounded almost offended. It surprised Nora. She'd never thought they would care or be interested in her extracurricular life.

"Trust me, it's boring. Six hours of arguing teenagers can get old real fast."

Charlie laughed. "Sounds like my life."

They said their goodbyes, with Nora promising to consider going to the memorial. Five minutes later, her mom was pulling up in front of the building. She climbed into the blacked-out BMW with the red interior accents she hated. Her mother had wanted dark purple interior trim. Her father had said otherwise.

"How was it?" her mother asked.

"Good. We won." Nora sat back, relaxing for the first time that day.

"Fantastic," her mom purred. "No better way to celebrate than going home and helping me bake cookies for the memorial on Monday."

Nora's shoulders tensed. So much for relaxing.

Chapter Five

Nora shaded her eyes from the sun as she looked around the church yard. She didn't know what or who she was looking for, but she hoped she'd find it soon. If she didn't, she'd have her mother to attend with. Beth Ann caught Nora's eye and she rushed to the girl's side. She could hear the clip of her mother's heels as she'd walked across the asphalt. She'd brought enough cookies to feed an army. Nora wanted no part in trying to snag some of the spotlight with her mother.

"Hey," Nora said as she casually walked up to Beth Ann. The two weren't close friends, weren't friends at all really. They had one common factor, the debate team. That's all Nora had in common with anyone at her school. Right now, she'd take it. Though she was the loner smart girl of the school, this was one event she didn't want to attend solo.

Beth fixed her black, knee-length skirt and tossed her stick straight black hair over her shoulder. "This is so terrible. I can't believe someone in our class is gone." Beth said it in a way that you might say it about a child being abducted; it was horrible, it was sad, but since it didn't hit home, she wasn't losing her mind with grief.

"I know," Nora said, wrapping her arms tighter around herself. This was where she struggled with her classmates – with people in general – small talk. She always managed to fumble over her words and say nothing of great importance.

Beth stayed by her side as they made their way into the sanctuary. Hundreds of people showed up for the memorial, including many teenagers and their parents. They'd all come to show their support to someone they didn't even know. It was all to keep up appearances.

"There's Reed," Beth said, gesturing toward the last pew. "I wonder how he's been holding up with all this mess."

Nora had been wondering the same thing. He crossed her mind several times as she'd scrolled through Instagram and read all the latest news reports. It was becoming her second hobby, checking for updates. "Are his parents not here with him?"

Beth huffed, as if she was trying to hold back a laugh. "Does he even have parents? I mean, seriously? Have you ever seen them?" She had a point. He'd been going to their school for six years, almost seven, and not once had his parents made an appearance. Anytime she'd seen him out in town, he was alone.

Beth waved her hands wildly in the air, almost hitting Nora in the face. When she looked around Beth's shoulder, who was a full foot taller than she was, Nora found out what the sudden squeal of enthusiasm was. Natalie and Brittany were standing off to the side, but once they saw Beth, they hurried across the chapel to get in line next to her. Nora became the odd one out, per usual. The other two acknowledged her with a polite smile, before the three broke out into their chatter, completely ignoring her.

Nora glanced back to the last pew where Reed was sitting. His head was bowed, as if he was praying, though Nora doubted that's what he was doing. She hadn't realized she was openly gawking at him until the lady behind her gently pushed her, urging her to go forward. The line had moved three whole pews forward while she'd been standing there wondering what Reed was thinking about.

She'd almost reached Brittany when, suddenly, she didn't want to be in line anymore. It was as if her body was moving on its own accord toward the back of the chapel. She slid onto the pew next to Reed, her heart pounding. Reed didn't move, didn't look up at her arrival. Neither one of them said anything and that would be okay had they been friends before, but now it felt awkward. Why had she gone back there?

Balling her hands into fists in her lap, she took a deep breath. "Where are your parents?" Inside, she groaned and beat her mind senseless. *If you came back here to make a fool of yourself and be a nosey posey, good job. You're succeeding.* Why had she gone back there?

Reed looked up then and there was a tilt to his lips, like he was trying not to smile but found her amusing. She could be quite the awkward clown. "Hello to you too, best friend."

Oh, wasn't he the funny one? "I get it. You don't owe me an explanation. We're not friends. Haha. Look at her coming over here to get nosey. Well, I'll have you know I came over here because…"

He started laughing, a full laugh that shook his shoulders. Nora could feel her face turning red. She started to get up, not willing to stay there and be mocked and laughed at when she was only trying to be nice. Yeah, she was a rambler and an easy target, but she wasn't a fool to stick around and take it. As soon as her feet pushed up and the upward motion of standing started to happen, Reed placed his hand on her arm, his face solemn.

"Don't go. To be honest, it is a little uncomfortable sitting back here by myself." He looked around the chapel. "Crazy how you can be in a packed place like this and feel like the only one here."

"That's one feeling I understand," she whispered. She did. She felt like that all the time. "How are you holding up?"

Reed shrugged and averted his eyes to the floor. It wasn't that he found their shoes fascinating, unless the scuff marks on his boots brought back fond memories. "I'm fine, which leads to the guilt. The guilt sucks."

Nora sucked in a sharp breath. Guilt? What did he have to feel guilty about? Her mind went to the murder. Was he about to confess something she didn't want to hear? Her heart rate spiked, not wanting to be a part of that. Taking a deep breath, she held still and hoped it wasn't about to come to some murder confession inside the school's chapel. She wasn't ready for that kind of friendship commitment with him. An officer standing in the corner caught her attention as he moved to get a bottle of water from one of the cheerleaders handing them out. "These things happen," she said, not really knowing what to say but feeling as if she needed to acknowledge what he said while also calculating how fast she could get to the officer.

"Not feeling bad about your supposed friend being dead happens?" He sat back against the pew, a smirk on his face. It made Nora's stomach tighten. "Nice to know. I feel better now."

Relief was a beautiful sigh that sung through her veins. No murder confession, thank God. "Oh. Were you two not close?" She'd always thought they were friends, but maybe they weren't. Maybe they were more like comrades in a school of people they had nothing in common with.

"Not really. Outside of school, we ran in different circles. His was a little… too intense for me." Reed rubbed at his right wrist. Nora saw a flash of scars before he pulled down his sleeve. It made her wonder if the circle Kyle had hung out with had done something to him.

She sat back in her seat and stared at the floor. It was her turn to find their shoes fascinating. "We can't help how we feel," she said, thinking of her own guilt she'd felt for not feeling sad about Kyle's death. "There's no reason to beat yourself up about it. You're showing your respects. Sometimes, that's enough."

Reed huffed a breath beside her. "It's true what they say about you then."

She adjusted her skirt and pushed a lock of her brown hair behind her ear before glancing up at him. She was afraid of what he was going to say to her. "They say a lot of things," she joked halfheartedly.

Reed nodded. "That's true, but I only believe the good stuff."

The speakers crackled, saving her from having to say something more. Her cheeks were burning hot, as was her body. She wasn't used to taking compliments, even if they were only implied and not said. She had to admit, he had a way with words. He also had a way of skirting around questions directed toward him, like that whole parent fiasco. While he had no obligation to answer her, he'd given no answer at all whether true or false.

"Ladies and gentlemen, we want to thank you for coming tonight." Nora spaced out as Principle Higgins droned on about the sadness the community felt. Kyle's mother and father sat on the front pew. His mother's head was bent as she wept for her son. His father sat straight, a hand on his wife's back.

Charlie's pep talk from this afternoon reminded Nora she needed to be profiling, just like the cops standing in the corners of the building. She was sure there were a few dressed as civilians throughout the crowd. Nora had already had the idea in mind, scoping out the crowd and looking for possible suspects, when Charlie had called her. Her and Liv were still not seeing eye to eye, so she'd had a lot of down time to look up how to profile a murderer at a funeral. Google, it's where it's at.

Liv had called her not long after she'd gotten home after the debate. She'd called again on Sunday and then once more Monday afternoon before the memorial. Liv had wanted to make it abundantly clear she did not have to go to the memorial if she felt uncomfortable. She reasoned as to why they weren't going, which made sense. She'd offered her support as best she could. The whole time, Nora had done everything to keep her friend complacent, except for telling her she agreed with Charlie on this one.

As she looked around the packed church; no one stood out to her. Students sat between their parents, appearing blank faced like they did during Monday morning announcements. The parents were zoned out, their arms draped protectively around their child. They were probably imagining what it was like to lose their child in such a way, or what that delicious smell was coming from the hall. A group of girls, whose parents were probably putting the feast together like her own mother, were sitting in the middle. They were huddled together, leaning on one another as if offering support. The whole thing made Nora sick.

"Are you okay?" Reed asked, leaning in close to her. Nora jumped, not expecting his proximity. "You look like a little tense."

'Little' was the understatement of the year. "Yeah," she answered and glanced over at him. Though it was a strange time to be noticing it, he had the deepest green eyes. "Feeling a little out of it." Lame, but efficient.

"Me too," he said before pulling away and sitting back up straight. "Hopefully Higgins won't take center stage for too long."

"Are you kidding me?" Nora whispered. "He thrives for this stuff. It's why he got elected as School Board Director. He's great at bullshitting."

Reed laughed and tried covering it with a cough. "You do realize you just cussed in a church, right?"

Nora's face flushed, and she covered her mouth to hide her smile. "Oops."

Once Higgins was done talking, the congregation stood and formed a line down the center of the aisle. Mr. and Mrs. Austin stood at the front. As people walked by, they shook Kyle's parents' hands and then made a bee line for the dining hall. Nora looked at her watch. "Forty-five minutes. That's like a new record for◌" Nora turned around and realized she was talking to thin air. Reed had disappeared.

She searched around the back of the chapel as she kept in step with the rest of the crowd, but she didn't see him anywhere. Where had he gone? The line moved in quiet formation with a few whispers about the floral designs or the sermon. Nora was lost in her own thoughts as she moved forward without thought. When she reached her mother, who was serving mashed potatoes, she snapped out of her spiral of thoughts. It was time to go.

"Oh, Nora, honey," her mother started, but Nora rushed ahead, interrupting her.

"Hey, Mom, this looks great, but I've got to go. A friend of mine is needing a ride home. This is all a little overwhelming for her." It was pathetic, but it was the best she could do right now. "I'll see you back home."

"Honey, wait," she heard her mom say, but she was already walking away. She didn't want to lie to her mother anymore than she needed. She wasn't used to this lying game, and the more that came out of her mouth, the more paranoid she became. Paranoid was becoming the new trend of her life.

Chapter Six

"Nora!" Her mom came storming in through her bedroom door, a furious mess of tangles and smeared makeup. She'd been up late last night, drinking, while her father stayed in the office yet again. "Will you please answer that blasted phone. It's been going off for hours."

Nora rolled over and glanced at the clock. It was almost six. Who would be calling her this early on a school day? Groaning, she apologized as her mom walked back out the door and down the hall. Her mom slammed her door shut, causing Nora to flinch. So, her father hadn't come home at all.

There were six missed calls and seven text messages, all from Liv. Not bothering with the messages, she called Liv back. It rang once before a frantic Liv answered.

"God, you sleep like a rock. I've been trying to call for almost an hour."

"I noticed. What's going on?" Nora rubbed the sleep out of her eyes and tried staying calm, which was hard to do considering how worked up Liv sounded.

"My uncle got a call this morning, bright and early. Someone vandalized the whole town." Liv sucked in a sharp breath, causing Nora's anxiety to spike. Why would someone vandalizing the town be of her concern? Unless… "Nora, it's bad. Someone posted hundreds, maybe thousands of posters all over town. It was a warning."

"A warning? A warning for what?" Nora whipped at the sweat building on her forehead. Suddenly, the morning chill she normally felt was gone.

"I just sent you a picture. Open it."

Nora put the phone on speaker and then went to her messages. Her hands were shaking and she missed the message icon twice before tapping it open.

It's a debate. Who's next? Better watch your back, you may be next.

There was a picture of a blacked-out gavel with outlines of people behind it.

Nora took the phone off speaker so her mom and Beth couldn't hear Liv. She stepped into her bathroom, shut the door, and turned on the water. Maybe it would be enough to drown out her voice. "Who would do this? Why?"

"I don't know, but it's bad. It's so bad, Nora. I've been freaking out all morning." Something rustled in the background, followed by a door closing. "Hang on, I'm going out to the tree house."

"The tree house?" Nora questioned.

"Yeah, my house is… cramped. It's where I go when I need some privacy." She grunted, probably climbing up into the tree. Nora had always wanted a tree house, but her dad had never taken the initiative to give her and Beth one, even though they had asked, begged, and pleaded for one. "It's really nice. You should come check it out sometime. Get out of that big mansion fluff. The splinters won't kill you, I promise."

Despite what was happening, Nora chuckled. Liv had no idea how little she worried about a splinter versus missing out on a whole lifetime of experiences. "When you say these posters were put up all over town, are you being accurate or exaggerating a little?" Nora hoped for the latter.

"I wish I was exaggerating. They were stapled to every electrical pole east, west, north, and south of town. It's bad."

Nora rubbed at her temple. She could already feel a headache forming. "You've said that."

"Charlie has already called me. She goes out with her mom in the mornings to deliver papers." For some reason, Nora couldn't picture Charlie delivering papers. It didn't fit her personality. Then again, no matter one's interest, they had to do whatever to reach their goals. Liv dropped her voice. "Nora, she thinks whoever did this was targeting you."

"Me? Why me?" If there was a person on the planet to draw enemies, it wouldn't be Nora. She didn't interact with too many people, and when she did, she was a coward. She didn't stand up for herself. She didn't argue. She was the good girl, the one people came to when they knew they could run her over. It didn't make sense.

"It was the mention of the debate. Neither one of us are in a debate club. That's not even offered at our school."

Nora's vision swam. Her breath was shallow. She had missed that part. *It's a debate.* And whoever had killed Kyle had chosen to do so because of her. Because it had been her night to choose and lead the crime until the others figured it out.

"I've gotta go," Nora whispered. Liv begged through the phone for Nora to wait, to talk to her, but she ignored her. She tapped the red button on her screen and Liv's voice died away.

Unable to hold herself up anymore, she slid down the cabinet until she felt the floor holding her up. What had she ever done to attract this kind of attention? No one, other than Liv and Charlie, knew she was a part of the murder club. Doubt once again webbed through her. Had they been too curious? Is that why they had reached out to her in the chat room, begging her to meet them in person? What, was this some kind of fun experiment to see what it really felt like to murder someone and get away with it?

Suddenly the room was too small and Nora couldn't breathe. Swaying from the pressure building up in her skull, she made her way to the front door. She grabbed her coat off the rack as she went for her mother's keys. She was fully aware she was still in her pajamas, but she didn't care. She needed some fresh air. She needed to move, to think.

The streets were quiet, with a fresh coat of snow from a storm that passed through the night before. Snow plows were out clearing the roads, but Nora wasn't waiting for them to be finished. She had to see the posters for herself. There had to be something to them, some kind of clue.

Cop cars littered the downtown area. They stood around a pole talking while one guy in a suit took a picture of the reason they'd been called to the scene. The posters. Nora took a side street, her heart pounding, her mind dizzy from all the fear coursing through her body. What if they put this all together and found her out? She hadn't done anything, not really, but it didn't matter. Not in the eyes of evidence, and right now, it was stacking up all around her.

She came out on Commerce Street. It was quiet, the shops still closed up tight. All the coffee shops were back out on Main Street, which was smart. People who were headed to work or school could stop in, grab what they needed, and get back on the road without having to navigate away from their route.

Snow blew into the car from the tree she parked under. Knowing her mother would kill her if she ruined her upholstery, she hurried and shut the door. The cold seeped in through her thin silk pajama pants, the snow easily soaking the thin fabric. Careful of her steps, she grabbed one of the posters off the pole. It ripped in the corner, leaving a small triangle of its existence.

Laying the paper on the passenger seat, she put the car in drive and headed out of town. She didn't know where she was going, but she knew she had to get away and think for a minute. Snow banks got higher the farther north she drove. Trees became thicker, and as the wind blew, it appeared as if it was snowing all over again.

Nora kept stealing glances at the poster. The outlines of a town of people. The large gavel looming in front of them. *Who's next?*

Her vision swam again and she jerked the car off to the side of the road. Covering her face, she practiced the deep breathing techniques she so often used on Beth. Deep breath. Focus on your heartbeat. Let it out slowly. Focus on the air leaving and entering your body. Deep breath. Repeat. Once her heartbeat was back to a normal rate and she could breathe without feeling as if she was about to suffocate, she looked up.

She was at the entrance point to the McKenzie Wilderness National Park. It had been so long since she had traveled up this far. Her mother used to bring her up here all the time during the summer, before her father went off the deep end and started sleeping at the office rather than their house. Beth was three the last time they came. It had been a hot summer day, one of those that you wanted to escape by finding the coolest place you could and hide away until the sun went down.

"How about we find us a cool place to relax," she had said with a wide smile. She grabbed up Beth and tossed her onto her hip. "I'm thinking a nice dip at the lodge would be perfect today."

Around Lake Placid, there were a lot of lodges. It was how the locals made a living. So many would come from the city, wanting to get a breath of cool air, but still wanting the luxuries they were so used to having. However, Nora knew what lodge her mother was talking about. It was the lodge where she had once worked as a receptionist. The same lodge where she met Nora's father and married him. Moose Lodge.

Nora and Beth had both jumped for joy before running out the door ready to go. It had been a beautiful day. Little did she know it would be one of their last to spend together as a happy family. After that, her father took a position at the firm, never stayed home, and became estranged from their mother who tried filling the void in her life by being the perfect housewife and finding solace through everyone else except her daughters.

How she missed those days. The quiet days. The laughter that broke the silence. The mom who cooed over their every move, rather than judge them. The dad who took the time to play golf with them at the country club. The parents who she felt she could talk to about anything. Now, when she needed them most in her life, they felt farther away than Mars.

Tears formed in her eyes as she picked up the poster. Who would be doing this to her? And why? An ache filled her chest. She needed someone to talk to about this, someone who may be able to lend her a helpful thought. But there was no one. Beth would lose sleep and her anxiety attacks would skyrocket. After all Beth had been through this last year, she couldn't put her sister through more. If something was to happen to Beth, if she was to have another psychotic break, she couldn't bear the thought of it being her fault. Once was enough for a lifetime. She'd barely managed to help get Beth semi-stable after she tortured her sister three years ago. She wasn't going to chance her being broken for the rest of her life.

Her mom and dad were out of the question. Maybe if they were the parents from her past, sure, but the ones she had now, nope. The only friends she had were Liv and

Charlie. That sad fact made her chest ache because now she wasn't sure they had been her friends at all.

Overwhelmed, she got out of the car and walked to the edge of the wood line. Snow was up to her ankles, chilling her fast. The wind was blowing, making the white powder fall from above. It was magical. The blue sky and falling snow, as the sun beat down on the blanket beneath her. If she could choose a moment to freeze time or to escape into forever, this would be it. An escape from all that she didn't know or understand. An escape from a person who wanted to frame her for murder.

~

It wasn't until well after lunch that she pulled back into the driveaway. The long drive had worn her down and all she could think about was going up to her room and relaxing for the rest of the evening. But as she got out of the car and saw Beth standing under the terrace waiting for her, she knew that wasn't going to happen. She was almost tempted to get back in the car and drive back to the lake.

"Where have you been? Mom's been freaking out since she got up."

Beth looked at her wrist, which wasn't sporting her watch, but she kept the ruse up anyway.

"So, what, an hour? That's not too bad."

"Ha, I wish. She's been up since seven," Beth hissed. "No sleep Mom on a hangover is no fun. No fun at all, Nora."

"I wasn't aware she was fun in any state." She tossed the keys between her hands as she leaned up against the terrace's wooden frame. It had recently been sealed to protect it from the weather's harsh conditions. The smell of the polyurethane was strong.

Beth crossed her arms and looked at Nora as if she didn't know who she was. The sad fact was, Nora didn't know if she knew who she was anymore either. "What has gotten into you?"

"Nothing." Oh yeah. She was a liar. That's who she was.

"Liar." If she only knew. "Tell me what's going on. Please. You tell me everything, or… you used to." She did. Nora told Beth everything. That was because Nora had no one else to tell. But she couldn't tell Beth about this. She couldn't. It would be too much for her to take.

"It's stupid," she said, stalling. What could she tell her sister that she may semi-believe?

"What do you always say to me?" Beth asked while nudging her with her elbow. "You always say 'If it's upsetting you, then it's not stupid. It means that it means something to you, even if it doesn't to anyone else'. Are you going to tell me that's all a lie? Because if you do, I may have to punch you in the face."

Nora wiped a tear off her cheek and laughed. Beth had punched her before for lying. It had hurt, a lot. She could only imagine how many times she would punch her once the truth all came out. "Remember those two girls you saw me with on Friday?" Beth nodded. "Well, I think that will be the one and only time you'll ever see them." As she said it, she realized it was something she needed to do. She needed to cut ties with Liv and Charlie for a while. She needed a break from them to think.

"Did you guys have a fight?" she asked.

"Something like that," Nora mumbled. "We aren't seeing eye to eye on a few things. They have their lives, I have mine. It's hard to explain." It was a terrible copout, one Nora felt guilty for even using as an excuse. She shouldn't be using her friends' lifestyles and hers as an excuse. It was sorry and selfish.

"Well, you better get ready for another not seeing eye to eye conversation. Mom is livid. More so than usual." Beth stepped over Cheese, their white cat with a little orange spot on her back. She had wandered into their neighborhood two years ago. When the neighbors started threatening to call animal control, Beth and Nora had claimed her. Their parents didn't put up too much of a fuss about it, other than her dad threatening to get rid of her if he found one turd outside the litter box. Beautiful thing was, he never had to worry about it. Cheese preferred letting loose out in the wild versus using a box with smell good pebbles. Beth opened the back door and Cheese darted inside.

"I bet she's more upset about the car than she is about me leaving." Nora stepped past Beth and into the house. The smell of coffee was thick. Her mom would be drinking coffee until the sun started to dip down to the horizon, then she'd switch to a glass with a stem.

"I'm not so sure about that. Your phone has been going off with messages and phone calls all morning. You should have taken it with you."

Nora froze. "Why?"

"She's going through it."

Nora rushed into the sitting room where she knew she would find her mother. It was her favorite place and she spent most of her time in that room. She'd never asked why, but Nora believed it was because of the perfect view of the driveway, not to mention the neighborhood. Her mother was curled up in the overstuffed, navy blue chair in the corner, a white pillow with blue polka dots on her lap supporting her arms that were holding Nora's phone.

"What are you doing?" Nora asked, furious. She'd never had to experience this before, not being trusted and having her things gone through like a common criminal. She didn't like it. Her body heated up, her skin feeling as if it had a fever, she was so furious. Nora reached for her phone and she was relieved to see her mother hadn't gotten past the password. Still, her mother pulled back, refusing to give Nora her phone back.

"What does it look like I'm doing?" her mother snapped. "I'm looking out for your best interests. You have exactly ten minutes to tell me where you have been before you have to go change out of that hideous outfit you have on and meet Gary."

Nora ignored the judgment her mom was throwing at her over her clothes. The thought of her daughter being out all morning in her pajamas was probably driving her mother crazy. *Good.* "Why am I meeting Gary?" What had she missed?

"He's being a responsible president." Her mom gave her a disdainful look. "Unlike the vice president who seems to be more content with making a debacle of herself."

Nora fisted her hands at her side. There was no point in arguing with her. Her mother made judgments off what she saw and made them reality in her mind, whether it was true or not.

Her mother glared at her. "I'm going to ask you one more time, where have you been?"

"I went for a drive. I've been feeling overwhelmed lately and I needed to clear my head." She knew her mom would think it had something to do with Kyle's death. It was a selfish ploy to play, but she needed her mom to back off. "I ended up at the lodge."

As she expected, her mother tensed at the mention of the lodge. She'd never said so out loud, but Nora and Beth believed her mom hated talking about the lodge because it was too painful. The lodge was once a place where they were happy, a family. It reminded her of how they used to be and how they were now, especially when it came to their dad.

Her mom seemed to physically shake the acknowledgment and whatever memories had surfaced out of her mind. "Did you know about the flyers around town before you took off?"

Nora thought of the flyer she'd thrown away in a dumpster at a gas station outside of town. She'd done it for this very reason; she didn't want any ties to them. She wanted to see them, to memorize every letter, but she hadn't wanted to be associated with them. It was too much of a risk. "What flyers?"

"Someone plastered flyers all over town last night," Beth said before their mother could answer. It was her way of reminding them she was still in the room. Beth always feared being forgotten, though Nora could never forget her sister. She was the only anchor in her life. "They seemed to be pointing the blame of Kyle's murder on the debate team."

"What?" Nora shouted. She was pretty proud of herself. She'd known this moment would come and she'd have to put on an act. The lies she'd told Beth and her mom would be crap then. Acting was not in her forte. "I don't understand."

Beth pulled out her phone and opened Instagram. When she turned her phone so Nora could see it, there was a picture of the flyer bright on her screen. Nora leaned in closer. "Do you think the police will take this seriously? It sounds ridiculous, like they're trying to frame the debate team."

"Those were my thoughts exactly," Beth said, locking her phone and putting it in her back pocket. She then gave their mother a pointed look. "She thinks otherwise."

"Why?" Her mother always had a different opinion compared to everyone else. She couldn't wait to hear what off the wall crap her mother would come up with this time.

"It's too obvious. I don't think that poor boy was murdered at all, but I do think someone is trying to use this as an opportunity to frame those they don't like." She gives Nora a pointed look, as if she was one who went around making a spectacle of herself. Her leaving this morning without a word to anyone was the wildest thing she'd done her whole life. Yes, she had sure racked up the enemies. "Which happens to be the debate team."

"Are you serious?" Nora asked, then looked to Beth, not believing what she was hearing. Their mother had officially lost her mind. "I'm not arguing the case for someone framing the debate team, I do believe that. But come on, Mom. You don't believe he was murdered? What else could have happened to a healthy seventeen-year-old boy?"

"Nora, Beth, let's leave your mama alone for now." Nora jumped at the sharp warning in Amy Hollis's tone as she came around the staircase, two cups of tea in hand. "Maybe later, huh? After your mama has had time to calm down now that you're home, Nora." A chill ran down Nora's spine. *What was Amy Hollis doing here?*

Nora gestured for Beth to follow her upstairs. She shut her door with a silent click and then turned on Beth. "What's she doing here?" It wasn't that Amy and her mom had never spoke before, but never had she come to their house. Stacey and Beth had never been friends, therefore never giving their moms reason to chit chat about sleepovers and parties together.

Beth shrugged and flopped down in the chair. "I don't know. She showed up this morning after word started to spread about the flyers. Debate team support group, maybe? I can see it happening."

It was a reasonable answer and she could see her mother orchestrating some support group in her living room. It would be the high she'd need. She took out her phone and sent Gary a quick message saying she would meet him at the coffee shop on Main Street after school, then tossed her phone aside.

"Do you think we are too hard on Mom?" she asked, sitting down next to Beth and pulling a blanket around them. She was suddenly exhausted.

Beth laid her head on Nora's shoulder. "Maybe." She yawned. "She's lonely."

Nora nodded, but didn't say anything. Her eyes were growing heavy as her body started to relax. "Beth," she whispered, almost asleep but curious about one more thing. "Why did you stay home from school today?"

Beth sighed and snuggled deeper into the blanket. "Because you're my sister and I had to make sure you were okay." A few breaths later, her light breathing and full weight on her shoulder let Nora know she was asleep.

Nora smiled. No matter what happened in the future, she knew Beth would always have her back.

Chapter Seven

It was bright outside. The ground glistened as the sun beat down on the snow. Nora pulled out her sunglasses as she sat down on the only dry bench on the school's grounds. Why the grounds-keepers didn't dust the snow off the benches like they did the school signs was beyond her. People didn't sit on the signs, nor did they read the school's motto as they walked by and hurried inside. To be fair, Nora was the only student who came out on sunny days, snow or no snow. Perhaps he didn't think she was worth the effort. Luckily, the sun did and had melted away the thin layer of snow that coated the wood this morning.

Resting her back against the bench, she tilted her head up toward the sun and soaked up the warmth it offered. Her mind began to wander, though she'd been fighting the urge to think about what Gary had said to her the day before when they'd met for coffee. He had been a jacked-up ball of nerves, hands shaking and movements twitchy. When he'd ordered his coffee, Nora had quickly leaned over the counter and told them to make it decaf. Gary was good about hyping himself up and staying there for a while. He didn't need the caffeinated help.

Once they'd settled down, Gary told her about the police coming to question him. How did he know Kyle? Did they talk often? Were they friends? How Gary would describe Kyle? Did Gary have a personal vendetta against Kyle for any reason? Had they ever had an altercation?

Nora had winced at the last question. She knew Gary could and never would harm anyone. He was a scrapping 110 pounds with glasses and was as polite as they came. The one thing he hated was confrontation, unless it was on a stage behind a podium. Problem was, Gary did have one confrontation that Nora could remember... and it was with Kyle.

They'd all been standing outside the cafeteria, waiting for Mr. Alvearies to come unlock the door so they could get the room ready for the debate the next day. Kyle happened to walk by the same time Gary snaughed. He was the best at snort laughing. Kyle had stopped and started poking fun of Gary. Then, he went on to ask about the debate club and asked why his application had been denied. This had been news to Nora. Never would she have thought someone like Kyle would join the debate team. Yet again, that was her mother's judgmental side shining bright. Gary, who was hurt over Kyle's comments about his laugh, had popped off saying, "You have to be smart enough to carry an A average to be on the team." The anger that passed over Kyle's face had scared Nora to the point she backed up and grabbed onto Stacey's arm for support. Seconds seemed to slip by as Kyle and Gary had a stare down. It was broken by Kyle coming up fast and hard, hitting Gary on the cheek and eye. Gary ended up having to get three stitches. Kyle got two weeks out of school suspension.

"You look deep in thought."

Nora startled, she was so deep in her thoughts. Shielding her eyes, she looked up to find Reed standing next to the bench. He was looking down at her with amusement in his eyes.

"Mind if I join you?" he asked. She had to admit, he was brave. If someone had been creepily staring up at her the way she had been him, she'd have turned and left.

She slid over and made room for him on the dry side of the bench. "I didn't know you came outside during lunch."

"I don't. This is a first for me." He rubbed his hands together. "Kyle and I used to hang out in the music room. He'd play on the guitar while I played my PSP."

Heat rose up to Nora's cheeks. "What brought you out here today then?"

A half smile crinkled his left eye. "You." His attention then went across the street. "Well, and the fact that the music room no longer seems a fit place to hang out. Considering I have no friends at this school and you're the only one willing to talk to me, I thought I'd give it a shot."

"Funny, I feel the exact same way around here." She was shocked she admitted it to him, but it was the truth. Ever since Beth had her incident things had changed big time for Nora. Her best friend Lacey had moved and everyone else kept her at arm's length, as if she might do the same as Beth had.

He tilted his head and looked at her with a glint in his eyes she didn't understand. "Their loss."

Nora's skin was on fire. Was he flirting with her?

"So," he said, rubbing his hands together again and puffing out a big ball of steamy breath. "Tell me, what are you always so deep in thought about?"

This time Nora grew warm for a whole different reason. Doubt started worming a hole into her mind. Reed was Kyle's supposed friend. She was sure he'd seen the flyers all around town yesterday. Was he here fishing for information rather than that supposed story he'd just fed her?

I'm starting to sound like a paranoid old lady. First Liv and Charlie, now Reed.

She decided to go with the truth. Lies only buried a person further and further into trouble. That was something she was learning with Beth real fast. Her parents may buy the lines she fed them, but not Beth. She was always looking at Nora now with skepticism.

"I'm sure you noticed the new decorations all over town yesterday."

Reed nodded. "I thought it was rather tacky."

It was tacky. Not only of the person who did it, but also the way they had been put together. It wasn't something you'd see from a computer savvy person for sure. The details and pictures had a lot of pixel details in them. Most computer programs don't have that issue anymore, unless you're trying to rip someone off and steal their content. Then someone might run into a pixel issue.

"Something was definitely off about it." It was a lame attempt for a response, but it was the best she could do. "Gary was freaking out about it."

"Gary?" Reed looked down at the snow, thoughtful.

"He's the president of the debate team," Nora prompted.

Reed snapped his fingers. "That's right. The next Einstein."

"I wouldn't go that far," Nora joked. Gary was smart, but he wasn't as smart as most people believed him to be. She'd caught him on more than one occasion cheating on tests. It was common, something a lot of students did to achieve those high application scores. "Gary has his faults."

"I wouldn't know," Reed said. "I'm only going off what Kyle said about the guy."

Nora thought about the incident between Kyle and Gary. "No love lost between those two."

Reed snorted. "That's for sure."

"After the flyers were found, Gary called together the debate team during lunch after being questioned by the police during fourth period. I wasn't here so we met for coffee after school." Nora picked at a loose thread in her coat. It sounded crazy in her mind, but she could swear she saw Reed tense next to her at the mention of Gary and her meeting for coffee. "He was warning us about the questions the police were asking. I think he was also giving everyone a chance to... I don't know... confess." Why did she feel so comfortable talking to him? The answer wasn't clear, but she found herself continuing without question. "It was almost like he was fishing."

"The cops could have put him up to it." A drop of water from the ice melting on the tree branch above them landed on Reed's jacket and traveled the length of his arm. Reed watched the trail it made, almost absently. "They do that from time to time, try to get someone from the inside to turn on everyone else."

"How would you know?" She hated the question and ease she felt at asking. Hated the doubt and red flag flying high in her mind now. It was none of her business and he had no reason to tell her about his past. Oh, but how she wanted to know.

He leaned in close, his lips close to her ears. "Some secrets are not mine to share." When he pulled away, a chill ran down her spine. When he saw the panic widening her eyes, he started laughing. "I'm joking. Have you not watched *NCIS* or *Law and Order*?"

Fresh air was welcomed into her lungs as she took a deep, relieved breath. She was sure he thought his closeness had caused her momentary shock. It had been a little bit. Okay, it had obviously been more than she would like to admit.

"It's a smart move," he said when she just continued to sit there saying nothing. "If someone murdered Kyle from the debate team, they'd be more likely to tell him first than a random adult stranger."

"That's true." She thought back to the way he was acting. *Had he been wearing a wire?* "I'm hoping they close the case soon, whether it's someone I know or not. I'm tired of walking around and looking over my shoulder."

"Do you think it was someone that goes here at the Academy?"

The question threw Nora. She'd been considering it, but she hadn't thought anyone else would be. It was a big speculation, one she couldn't see anyone in their class committing. That was the thing about murderers, sometimes they're hard to suspect until it's too late.

"I'm not sure. At first, no. I thought it might be some gang or person Kyle got mixed up with outside of school. Then the flyers were put up all over town and now I'm not so sure." The truth was, she was afraid it was someone in her class. Someone who had found her out and was framing her for failure. Why? She didn't know, but it's what it felt like. And if she didn't figure something out soon, she was going to go mad with paranoia.

They sat quietly for a few minutes. Nora checked her watch to see they only had seven minutes left of lunch. What was she going to say to fill the seven-minute void?

Luckily, Reed helped with that. "You weren't here yesterday." It wasn't exactly a question, more of an observation, but Nora felt inclined to explain.

"The flyers kind of freaked me out. The accusation was pretty clear for anyone who's lived in this town long enough. I knew I couldn't handle coming to school, so I went for a drive through the mountains. I ended up going to one of my favorite places from my childhood." She cringed inwardly. She'd meant to tell him she couldn't handle it so she'd gone for a drive. Mentioning her favorite childhood place was a bit of an overshare, or at least that's what all the *How to Be Social* books she read suggested. Keep it simple, give the other person a token of yourself, but keep the focus on them. People love to talk about themselves, not hear about you. The books had become a staple in her life after Beth's freak out and Lacey leaving. After a while, she dropped it all and said screw it. She could live without friends. Everyone already thought she was a stuck-up snob on the brink of a psychotic break, when really she was shy and striving to live up to her father's expectations. Now, with Reed trying to make small talk, she tried digging up every tip and step-by-step chapter the books offered.

Reed relaxed a little more on the bench. "That must have been nice. I don't have a favorite childhood place."

That took Nora by surprise. Of course, she lived in a fantasy world most her life where every character in every book she read had a favorite childhood spot. "There must have been somewhere." She pushed, not for her sake but for his. He may not have realized it, but she was sure there was somewhere he thought of with a sense of comfort.

He looked thoughtful for a minute. "Well, there was an old tree in my back yard I used to gaze at fondly." He smiled over at her. "Does that count?"

She couldn't help but smile back. "Definitely."

The school's singsong chime went off, signaling the end of lunch. *Dang, we were just starting to get to know each other.* Gathering up her things, she started to get up when Reed handed her a piece of paper. "My number. Call me."

He slung his backpack over one shoulder and took off without a glance back as Nora prayed her heart wouldn't explode in her chest. If anything gave her anxiety, it was the expectations that followed when someone gave her their number. She'd panicked for three days after getting

Liv's number before sending a nonchalant greeting. Building up to send a 'Hey' to Reed was going to be a lot worse.

She let him get to the doors before she followed. A smile crept across her face as warmth filled her cheeks. A new flutter filled her stomach as she pulled open the door and headed back into the hallway. Unlike this morning when she'd been a ball of nerves, it had nothing to do with the flyers. It wasn't until the intercom dinged and her name was blared over the speaker for all to hear that the knot in her stomach changed to dread. All eyes turned on her as she stood there, staring at the speaker above the rows of lockers that lined the wall.

Grabbing her books for her next class, she ducked her head and did her best to ignore the stares as she made her way to the office. She could only imagine what everyone was thinking. *I knew she would break one day. She's worse than her sister. The mystery is over.* One was brave enough to voice that opinion. "Guess the crazy runs thick in that family after all." She turned to see it was Braxton Woods, the swimming champ of the Academy and Beth Ann's boyfriend. Beth Ann was standing next to him, but she did little to stand up for Nora's honor. The only thing her debate team member did was nudge him with her elbow and gesture the other way toward class. With a shake of his head, he followed.

Nora kept her head low as she made her way to the office. Once inside, the relief she was hoping to find didn't come. She'd been hoping they needed her for something minimal, a scholarship application or debate team report. When she saw two police officers standing inside Principal Higgin's office, she was sure she was going to pass out. Gary had warned her, she'd been prepared, yet, with her heart racing and light sheen of sweet building on her neck, she felt blindsided – like it all had been a joke.

"Ah, Ms. Fletcher, I'll let Principal Higgin's know you are here. Why don't you have a seat." She gestured to the two red cushioned chairs against the wall.

Nora tried to mind her manners and thank Mrs. Vass, but it wasn't happening. Her throat was clenched tight and she could barely manage to swallow. Two magazines were centered on the black wooden table placed between the chairs. One was for parent's titled *Raising Your Best*. Yeah, that didn't sound overbearing at all. The other was for kids titled *Being Your Best Academic Self*. What a pair those two make.

Taking a deep breath and trying to calm herself, Nora had just started to relax when Higgin's door opened and her muscles retracted back as tight as they could go. She was stiff and wasn't sure she was going to be able to stand, let alone speak.

"Ms. Fletcher, come on into my office."

She commanded her body to move and was proud of the progress it made. That is until she reached the doorway, gagged, and almost fell on her face.

"Are you okay?" Higgins asked while leading her to a chair.

"Fine," she mumbled, embarrassed out of her mind. Who almost vomits and trips over themselves while trying to play it cool in front of the police, guilty people that's who. Except, she wasn't guilty. The problem was going to be convincing them of that.

"Hello, Ms. Fletcher. I'm Detective Taylor, this is my partner Detective Garcia." The woman looked at Nora as if she already had her pegged as the criminal. Nora's lunch began to rise again as another wave of warmth passed through her. It took everything she had to fight back the bile rising in her throat.

"Nice to meet you," she stammered. She was lucky to have done that.

Detective Taylor took a seat next to her in the matching cherry wood chair. Detective Garcia continued to stand, like a vulture waiting to pounce on its prey. "We talked to Mr. Higgins and it seems you're quite the academic student. You've got a clean record, never been in any altercations, and have quite the scores on your SATs."

Nora wanted to say thank you, but she knew there was a catch building. She could feel it in the air. She was waiting for the 'with everything lining up for you, why would you commit murder?' question. It was coming, or something close to the accusation as they could get. Again, her stomach rolled.

"We almost didn't question you. However, there was one student who gave us reason to pause and rethink that decision. She said you had an altercation with Kyle the day he was murdered. Can you confirm or deny that?" His brown eyes were gentle as he looked across to Nora. She was sure he could hear her heart beating wildly. Garcia had no such sympathy.

When it didn't seem like she was going to answer, Higgins placed his hand on her shoulder causing her to flinch. "It's okay, Nora. You're under no judgment here." It was a good thing people didn't really get struck by lightening for lying. If they did, the heavy hand on her shoulder would become dust in seconds. If she wasn't under judgment, she wouldn't be here.

Her throat burned as she opened her mouth to answer. "I did run into Kyle that day. He was standing next to his locker as I was leaving. The hallways were empty so I was an easy target for him."

"Easy target?" Taylor questioned. The was a pinch of concern on his face.

Why did I say that? "Kyle liked to give others a hard time. I was pretty good about avoiding him, but I didn't see him that day until I was already passing him." She didn't want to speak ill of the dead or sound as if she was pointing the blame on him. One point she remembered from one of the profiling books she'd read, the guilty will sometimes try to play victim. Is that what she sounded like?

"So, Kyle was a bully?" Garcia asked. Great. She was jumping on the guilty victim ploy tactic fast. Nora was going to have to back paddle. Hard.

"No," she lied. "I think he was standing his ground and protecting himself. I never saw him intentionally go out of his way to be mean to anyone. He might say something if he noticed it, like he did with me that day, but he didn't just see targets and pounce." *Oh God, Nora, shut up.* Maybe she should look into the medical field like her parents wanted. At least then she wouldn't have to talk to people as often, or build terrible lies no one believed. She could tell by the skepticism in Garcia's eyes she didn't believe her.

"Why would he have to stand his ground?" Taylor asked.

Nora hunched in on herself. She didn't want to say it. God, she didn't want to say it. She was going to have to say it. *Dammit.* "He wasn't… from this side of town. I think he felt a need to shield himself from that fact."

"So, you're saying because he wasn't rich he didn't fit in," Garcia snapped.

"That's not…" Nora rubbed her hands over her face. Anger built in her chest, and like the bile had earlier, it was rising up inside her body. "I've lived here my whole life, went to the same school, and guess what, I don't fit in either. So no, it had nothing to do with money, though I believe Kyle felt it did." The outburst had come fast and loud, but she sat back, glad to have spoken her mind. The only part she'd left out was the fact that Kyle was a bully and she wasn't.

Out of the corner of her eye, she had slowly watched Higgins retreat. Nora accusing the school of being biased on income was not an image he wanted portrayed. "I'd like to clarify, we don't have a problem here☐"

"We can discuss that later, Mr. Higgins," Taylor interrupted. "I have a few more questions for Nora. Can you tell me what happened in the hallway? The day Kyle was killed."

She liked the subtle reminder he threw in there. It was just the right touch to set her back on the frantic edge. Taking a deep breath, she did her best to recall every detail of that day. "I was at my locker with Stacey Hollis, who was giving me a hard time about missing the debate meeting. Yes, I snapped at her, but I've never missed a meeting in my life, and she acted like it was some big deal because I had something else to do that day."

"What did you have to do?" Garcia asked.

Nora tried to hide the cringe that took over her body. "I had to meet my sister after school." She hated bringing her sister into the mix. Beth being questioned by the police could be a lot for her to handle. Nora also knew Beth would catch onto the lie and cover for her, though she would have some questions of her own later.

Taylor jotted something down in his notebook. "What happened after you left Stacey?"

"I was walking out and passed Kyle in the hall. He made a remark about me standing up for myself, said he didn't think I had it in me. I snapped at him, like I had to Stacey and walked out the door." She knew it wasn't going to be as simple as that. There would be more questions, but relief flooded through her. She felt like the worst was over, even if it was a beautiful lie she was telling herself.

"Do you remember what you said to him?" Garcia asked.

Nora tried recalling what she'd said to Kyle but couldn't remember her exact words. What did they expect of her? It was almost a week ago. "I said something along the lines of being fed up or pushed to a limit. I really don't remember."

Garcia arched a brow and folded her arms over her chest. Taylor jotted something else down in his notebook. Nora wanted to snatch the thin writing pad out of his hands and run. What was he writing about her?

"Did you see Kyle again after that?" Taylor asked.

Nora shook her head. "I met my sister and went home. We heard the news about Kyle later that night."

They asked her a few more questions. Was there anyone in the hall with him? Yes, Reed. Had her and Kyle ever exchanged heated words before? No. Did she ever feel like Kyle was a threat to her? No. Did she have any reason to want to harm him? Double no.

As she was getting up to leave, she had to wonder if this line of questioning really worked. Was there not a better method? Who would come out and say, yes, I wanted to kill him? Then again, it takes only one mistake, one lie, to slip up, and they've got you. It's why they ask the same questions over and over. She guessed the questioning had its reasons, no matter how ridiculous it seemed.

She was almost out the door when Garcia called out her name. Nora glanced back over her shoulder. "We'll be in touch." The threat was loud and clear. Nora wasn't out of the crosshairs yet.

Chapter Eight

Beth had just placed the plates on the kitchen table while Nora carried in the silverware when the front door bell rang. Before either one of them could react, a furious precession of dings followed. Nora abandoned the silverware in a pile on the table and rushed to the door. Amy and Stacey Hollis greeted her on the other side with worried expressions. Tear streaks stained Stacey face.

"Mrs. Hollis is everything okay?" The only other time she had seen Stacey this upset was when her grandmother died. Even when Amy had left her husband of fifteen years two year ago, the girl hadn't been this upset. Amy drained her husband dry and the two had been happy frolicking around the neighborhood ever since.

"It's awful, just awful." Amy stepped inside and shrugged off her coat. Stacey opted to keep hers on and followed her mother into the dining room. Beth stood there awkwardly and narrowed her eyes on Nora with a 'what do I do?' glare over their shoulders. She was looking to the wrong person for answers. She still didn't know what this was all about.

Thankfully, her mom came to the rescue. "Amy, Stacey, what's happened? Is everything okay?" Mom rushed to Amy's side and wrapped her arms around her shoulders protectively.

"It's just awful, Cathy. How can they suspect our children of such a horrible situation?" Amy shuddered and reached up to put her hand over Cathy's.

Is she being for real? Nora looked at her sister and rolled her eyes. They'd always joked about how dramatic everyone was around the neighborhood. Northern Ridge Estate, Home of the Paranoid Drama Elites. Amy was doing a wonderful job filling the shoes. Nora had been proud of her mother, who had taken hearing her daughter being interviewed by the police with a strong backbone. She didn't scream, freak out, cry, or grab her phone to call everyone in her contacts like Nora had been expecting. Instead, she had calmly called Nora's father, told him what happened, asked him to contact their lawyer for a heads up, and asked what Nora wanted for dinner. It had been calm, and oddly enough, a comfort that Nora welcomed. She didn't want the tears or hugs of a wailing person grabbing onto her, proclaiming she didn't know what they were going to do. She needed someone to help her take control and steady the rocky water she felt she was trying to navigate. That's exactly what Cathy had done, for the first time in a long time.

Amy wailed on and on about how unfair it was of the police to question Stacey without her consent. Nora's dad then assured the hysterical woman that the detectives had done no wrong, but that if Stacey gets questioned in the future she can refuse to answer until her mom or lawyer was present. He had drilled the same reassurance into Nora when he'd come home from the office early. It was the first time in a long time, and it surprised not only Nora, but her mother as well. He'd sat them all down in the sitting room, told them they had nothing to worry about; the police were gathering evidence and that required asking questions, but that in the future he wanted her to request he be present. When a tear had escaped down Nora's mother's face, she'd thought it was because of the predicament of the murder. Then, as her mother smiled over at her father, Nora realized it was her father's presence. Simple as that.

"Should I have a lawyer speak with Stacey?" Amy asked, a sob catching in her throat. Nora's father sat down at the table and rested his laced hands in front of him. Going into business mode, her father began his spill on how it wouldn't hurt to have a lawyer in the know of what was happening and why. It was a speech Nora had heard often. "Don't keep the person who can save your ass in the dark." Made sense.

Nora's phone vibrated in her pocket. She pulled it out to find a text from Beth.

Beth: I bet that's why she's here. Free legal advice.

Nora rolled her eyes. There's was no doubt in her mind that's why she was here.

"Can I be excused?" Nora asked. The last thing she wanted to do was sit at the dining room table and watch Amy cry for the next hour or two. She had a paper to write, not to mention a mystery to solve.

"Sure, honey. Beth, why don't you go upstairs with your sister." Cathy glanced over at her daughters with gratitude, a silent thank you of understanding. Nora understood all too well. If she didn't escape, she was going to go mad. "The two of you order a pizza."

Nora had started for the staircase when Stacey caught her eye in the corner. She was huddled in on herself, her arms tightly wrapped around her torso. She looked sick, homely even, though Nora knew that wasn't the case. With a dramatic mother like hers, she was sure the girl didn't get comfort often. She didn't have a sister like Nora did. Without Beth, Nora would have lost her mind a long time ago. She could only hope Beth felt the same way.

"Stacey," she said, catching the other girl's attention. When she looked up, Nora gestured toward the stairs and motioned for her to follow. When they got up to her room, Stacey lost all control.

"I can't believe this is happening," she said, zooming around Nora to pace in the middle of the room. "How can they think I had anything to do with it?"

There was no hiding the groan that came out of Nora. She didn't do well with others freaking out. She reserved that for herself. "No one said you did it specifically."

Stacey threw her hands in the air. "They might as well have," she sobbed. "They treated me like a common criminal."

Beth snorted. "Really? You know how a common criminal is treated? Tell me, do handcuffs really hurt or is that just a movie thing?"

"Quit being a smartass, Beth," Stacey snapped. "I was terrified."

A headache was starting to pound behind Nora's eyes. She couldn't remember the last time she got a full night's sleep. "Did Gary not talk to you before the police did?" Nora had been freaked out when the police were questioning her, but she was sure she had a little more reason than Stacey. Stacey didn't have bread crumbs all around her feet.

"That doesn't matter. You can get the best pep talks in the world and still freak out when the moment presents itself." A slight sheen of sweat was building on Stacey's forehead. She took off her jacket and tossed it over the back of the desk chair. "Doesn't this scare you at all, Nora. I mean, all eyes are on the debate team."

Nora was scared, but she had her own set of reasons which had nothing to do with the debate team. "I don't know. It was a bold public statement, sure, but I think it was for distraction. If someone really did kill Kyle, they're doing the typical throw some clues at other people game." When Stacey's face went pale, as if she was surprised Nora knew so much, Nora gestured between herself and Beth. "We know a thing or two about law."

The reminder eased Stacey's surprise. "That's right. I forget your dad is an estate lawyer." Nora held her tongue and decided not to make mention they weren't exactly the closest of friends. Stacey collapsed onto Nora's bed. "I'm so scared this is going to fall back on me, even though I didn't do anything wrong."

Beth folded her hands, rested her chin on her intertwined fingers, and batted her eyelashes at Stacey. It was clear Beth didn't care for the other girl. "If you didn't do anything wrong, how could they frame you for murder?"

"It happens all the time," Stacey sobbed. Nora grabbed a tissue and handed it to her. The last thing she wanted was her snot all over the bed. "One tiff and an accusation and the next thing a person knows they are behind jail for no reason."

"It's *behind bars*," Beth corrected.

Stacey cut her eyes over at her and started to say something, but Nora jumped in to stop the argument. "What do you mean by one tiff?" Her phone buzzed in her pocket. She pulled it out to find a text from Liv.

Liv: Why are you ignoring me on chat? What's up?

Nora shoved the phone back in her pocket, ignoring Liv again. She didn't know what to tell her. *Sorry, but I'm not sure I can trust you right now.* She could already picture the outburst Liv and Charlie would have if she told them the truth. She still had some thinking to do about the whole situation. Add that to the growing list of reasons as to why she was losing sleep.

"Last Monday Kyle and I got into an argument," Stacey explained. Her face turned a shade redder as she focused her attention on the floor. "Before you ask, it was about me kissing him at a bonfire by the lake last Saturday."

Nora's eyes widened. Stacey was a picky one, so picky she'd once told a Niles Owen that if he cut his hair a certain way she'd go out with him. He'd gotten the cut. She ended up breaking up with him two weeks later because their auras didn't match or some crap. Imagining her with Kyle was almost impossible. Almost. "I knew you had a darker streak in you," Nora jabbed. "You like them wild and sexy, huh?"

Stacey's face was full on red. "I like the challenging aspect of it, yes. I also know this is just high school and the chances of any relationship lasting outside of it is less than ten percent." She stood, unable to sit still while she spilled her embarrassing secret. "The thing was, I didn't want him to tell anyone we'd made out at the party. No one saw us, so I was trying to get him to keep it a secret. I said it would make it more fun. Kyle got pissed, said I was using him as a boy toy but one I was ashamed of."

"When the kettle's black…" Beth said, leaving the rest unspoken. Stacey couldn't deny that's what was going on either.

"Just because it was true doesn't mean I didn't want to spare his feelings. Plus, he was good. Real good." Stacey got lost in her head for a minute. Nora didn't even want to imagine what she was thinking about. After a few awkward seconds, Nora snapped her fingers in front of Stacey's face. "Oh, right. Anyway, we got into it in the hallway and he never spoke to me again."

"I'm guessing he had a serious crush on you then, because most guys who have no emotional bond with the other person would be down for a secret affair. If it meant they were getting laid that is." Nora gasped and looked at her sister in shock. Beth shrugged. "Real life, Nora. I'm not five."

True. "I think it was more of an ego thing. Kyle was having a hard time with not fitting in at Pinewood."

Stacey looked confused. "What do you mean? I was feeding his ego well."

Gag. "For one, gross. For two, I meant with you rejecting him in public. Kyle wanted to be one of the elites, bad. He felt inferior to everyone else because he didn't have the same financial status or address as the rest of us."

"How do you know?" Stacey asked.

Nora thought back to the few incidents she knew about Kyle. Factor in the remarks Reed had made and it wasn't hard to figure out. "Think about it. He tried getting on the debate team. Denied. He tried out for tennis. Denied. He tried dating other girls besides you. Denied. Him and Reed were the only students in that school on a scholarship and neither one of them could make a step ahead like the rest of us."

"Probably because his parents couldn't make a hefty donation like everyone else's," Beth added.

Nora snapped her fingers. "Good point. Kyle always tried but no matter how hard he tried, he got denied. Which is exactly what you did when you wanted to 'keep it a secret'." Nora loved the angry face Stacey gave her when she used air quotes. She knew it drove the other girl crazy. "Kyle was sick and tired of being forgotten. He tried shielding himself from it, but sometimes that didn't always work."

"Oh my god," Stacey fell back down onto the bed. Not for the first time Nora wondered if Stacey's mom was done boohooing to her mother. She was over Stacey's drama. "So, they can use my argument against me and say I murdered him because I didn't want others to know about us."

"Awe," Beth drawled. "She really is a self-centered thing, isn't she?"

Nora snaughled at Beth's cooing tone. She wasn't wrong either. After everything Nora had told her about Kyle and how Stacey treating him that way had been wrong on so many levels, she'd still come out of it only thinking about herself. Forget that Kyle is dead.

For the next hour, the girls entertained Stacey with some Netflix and pizza. When Amy called her from downstairs to tell her it's time to go, it takes everything in Nora not to push her out the door. Once they hear the front door close, Beth and Nora breath a sigh of relief.

"I never thought she was going to leave," Nora remarked.

"I don't see how you do it," Beth said.

"What?"

"Keep up with her," she said, gesturing toward the door. "I couldn't do it."

Nora laughed. "I'm good at blocking her out. Plus, she doesn't push me too hard. I am the vice president after all. I can suggest we keep her off the team."

Beth called it a night, claiming all the excitement had wore her down. What she really needed was some quiet time to process and regroup. The explanation the therapist had given Nora and her parents was that Beth's mind was wired a little different. Then he went on to explain the differences between introverts and extroverts to them. By the time he was finished, Nora was sure she was an introvert too. Prefers being alone. Creators and thinkers who when in a large group need to chill out alone to process and unwind. Sounded like her. The therapist had to reassure their mother several times that it was a normal part of human development. Nora was sure her mother still didn't believe him.

That's what Beth needed right now, though. Time to process. Nora was waiting for her to figure out the lies, the flyers, and what happened with the police, piece it all together, and come knocking on her door demanding answers.

Nora tried to relax with a book, but her mind was too keyed up. From Reed sitting with her at lunch to the police to Stacey ugly crying in her bedroom, her mind was a spinning tangle of thought. She thought about Reed and his invitation for her to call him. What would she say? Did she send a simple hey or did it need to be more complex than that?

As she was contemplating it, her phone buzzed in her hands. It was another text from Liz.

Liz: Charlie has a theory about the killer. Meet us at the library tomorrow after school?

She typed a quick, **I'll be there.** Then she set her phone aside and stared at her ceiling. Who had she been kidding, she wasn't going to text Reed. It was nothing but a fantasy, one she smiled about yet felt the deep seed of sadness in her soul. Why did she have to be so spineless sometimes?

She hadn't realized she'd dozed off until her mother was shaking her awake. She glanced at the clock to find it was after eleven. "What's going on?" she mumbled, while scooting up toward the headboard.

"Maybe you can explain this to me," her mom snapped and tossed a piece of paper onto Nora's lap.

Confused, Nora picked it up to find it was a picture. Her eyes widened when she saw herself sitting across from Liv. "Where did you get this?" she asked, flinging the covers off her legs, her body suddenly warm. She got up from her bed and went to her desk to flip on the lamp.

"Someone left an envelope with this picture and a letter." Her mom reached in the pocket of her rob and pulled out a piece of paper. She thrust it out toward Nora.

With sweaty palms, Nora took it. *Do you know what your daughter has been up to?* "What's this supposed to mean?" It was a stupid question. It was clear what it meant. What Nora didn't understand was who would this? And who had been following her around to take this picture? She'd told no one about where she went on Thursday's.

Maybe Liv and Charlie had. Ease over the idea of Charlie and Liv being involved started to lift off her chest. It was proof they couldn't have been. It took zero point one seconds for doubt to creep its ugly head back into the picture. They could have had someone take the picture for them.

"You tell me, young lady. Obviously, it's something bad enough your friends wanted me to find out." Friends, ha. The last person her mother had to worry about were her so-called Pinewood friends. They wouldn't care if Nora had been the one floating in the lake.

"It's nothing. I was helping tutor some kids from West for community credits. I didn't feel comfortable going to their school alone, so I requested for our meetings to be held at the public library." Another lie she was going to have to keep up with. All in the sake of protecting who, Charlie and Liv? What if they were the ones behind all this?

"You could have told us," her mother snapped.

Nora half-heartedly laughed. If she had been tutoring kids from West at the public library for real, she wasn't sure she'd tell her mom and dad even then. She hated how they judged her every move. "That's the thing, Mom. I can't tell you anything without being threatened with a psychiatrist. So, no, I couldn't tell you."

The blow was harsh but true, and it hit her mom like a slap in the face. Nora didn't regret it, though. She needed to let out some of the pressure building inside of her.

"You could..." Her mom trailed off, unable to bring herself to disagree with a lie. She knew it was true. Instead, she turned for the door. As she was about to shut it, she looked back over her shoulder. "Good night, Nora." The softness in her tone and tears brimming in her eyes twisted Nora's stomach.

After her mother left, Nora sat down at her desk with the picture in hand. Who had left this on her porch for her parents? Better yet, why? It wasn't anything incriminating. Whoever did it had to have known her parents would react the way they had. Well, at least her mother. She should have asked if her father knew before going off the rails.

Unable to go back to sleep, she pulled out her notebook to jotted down the picture. She'd been keeping a timeline with possible suspects named at the bottom. After adding the date and description of the picture to the timeline, she moved her pen to the bottom of the paper. She added Stacey Hollis to the list.

Chapter Nine

The smell of bacon wafted through the bathroom door as Nora finished brushing out her hair. Her mouth watered. She couldn't remember the last time she'd eaten bacon. Hurrying to finish her morning routine, she ran downstairs to find her dad standing at the stove. Beth came in through the other entryway, saw her dad, and with wide eyes looked to Nora. They both rushed to the window.

"Have you heard any news this morning?" Beth asked while scanning the sky.

"Nothing important. Anything on Instagram?" Nora asked, looking down the street to see if a tidal wave was off in the distance or maybe a wall of lava. For surely doomsday had come.

"Melanie Day's freckled I'm-so-fake-it'll-make-you-sick face, but that's an everyday occurrence. I'd be worried if I didn't see her face." Nora laughed as she scanned the mountain ridges off in the distance. Everything looked fine. The sky was clear. The sun bright and melting the thin layer of snow still clinging to the grass.

Nora stepped back from the window. "I don't think Hell's froze over and doomsday doesn't seem to be upon us, so…" she trailed off, hoping the unknown would fill the gap itself.

"Divorce?" Beth chimed in.

From the kitchen her dad laughed. "You know, I like the imagination showed here, though it's at my expense." He whirled around, two plates in hand. His famous bacon rollups, loaded with cheese and eggs, with a side of toast filled the plate. Nora's mouth watered. She hadn't had his bacon rollups since they were kids. "It occurred to me yesterday with everything that is going on, not to mention Nora's outburst last night, that I may need to be around more."

"What's the catch?" Beth asked. It was a bold question, but Nora had been thinking the same thing. What was the catch? When Beth had her incident three years ago, been hospitalized for four days, and then put in therapy, he had stayed hard at it. He would take off for the occasional visit, but he'd make up for it by working late into the night. After all: *Fletcher's don't slack. We make sacrifices and get things done.*

"Ouch. I deserve that." He poured them a glass of OJ. "You know, I've always thought our family was forever. That I would get around to 'tomorrow' with you guys, but each day slipped by and you two are almost adults. I guess you can say Kyle's passing away and seeing his father at the office two days after Kyle's death, and then the threats made, well, it opened my eyes a little. As did your mom who let loose on me last night, after she talked to you, I might add," he said, winking at Nora.

Nora flinched. She hadn't known Kyle's father was seeking financial advice from her dad. She wasn't aware they were in a situation where it was even necessary. She wanted to question her father about it more but knew now wasn't the time. Now was for their family. She hadn't meant to cause a stir between her mother and father by losing control last night after seeing the picture. "I'm sorry, dad. I just▨"

"No," he interjected, "it's was an overdue conversation. I've always strived to do the best for my family and pushed you two to do the same. Problem was, what I saw as the best, as a sacrifice, was also destroying the family I wanted to take care of. I just wished your mother would have ripped me a new one a long time ago."

"Everything comes in the right timing, dear." Her mother walked into the kitchen, a smile on her face. Last night Nora had regretted yelling at her mother, but considering the outcome, she was kind of glad she did.

After breakfast, the girls left for school while their parents planned out a day together. There was the mention of stopping by the office, but only to grab dad's laptop so he could work from home for a few days. It was odd, but something Nora hoped they got used to.

"I like this," Beth said, right before they reached the gates of Pinewood Academy. "Walking every morning, I mean. It's nice."

Nora hadn't thought about it until now, but her and Beth had taken to walking since Liv and Charlie came to their house the morning after Kyle's death. "It is nice." It was also therapeutic, which was why she'd been doing it. She needed the fresh air and time to think before being thrust into the hallways to be gawked at. This last week had been a sour blast to three years ago when she was treated like a thin sheet of glass.

"I hope this sticks," Beth said. Without having to explain, Nora knew what she meant. Their mom and dad's chipper attitude.

"Me too."

Nora spent the rest of the day caught between worry and hope for her parents, all while ignoring the whispers around her. It'd been a long time since they'd been a family not pretending to be a family. She hated to admit it, felt cheesy for even thinking it, but she wanted her family back whole. Not just the image that hung on the wall and that was sent out at Christmas, but the real family behind closed doors that no one else saw.

When the last bell rang, she leaped from her chair and was the first to her locker. She was done with the day. It seemed like everywhere she went eyes were following, along with the whispers. She wasn't sure but she thought she heard something about a poll for who you thought was the debate killer. She was sure she was leading that vote.

Her stomach filled with knots as she stepped onto the sidewalk and headed for town, not home. She hadn't seen Charlie and Liv in a few days, having been ignoring them.

Nora's walk to the library was quiet. Her thoughts swirled between excuses not to go and what she was going to say to Liv and Charlie. She still didn't know what to think. Were they involved in the murder or not? Liv had been the one to call and tell her about Kyle's death. They'd both called to give her advice on how to handle the memorial. They'd both called to check on her every day until she started ignoring them. What did that say about her as a friend? Maybe everyone was right. Maybe she was crazy like Beth.

Inside the library, she found Liv and Charlie quietly tucked away in their usual corner. Liv sat up, seeming happy to see her. Charlie, on the other hand, didn't seem to care at all. "Surprised you showed up," she said, still flipping through a Vogue magazine. "The way you've been ignoring us, I figured you'd wrote us off as too much trouble."

"Do I have a reason to do that?" She met Charlie's stare and demanded herself not to budge. After five deep breaths, she continued, "Because I don't. If you hadn't noticed, I've been under some deep surveillance thanks to those stupid flyers. Then there's my parents…" She didn't know what to say about the sudden change and didn't want to dive into it, so she let the implications fall where they may. "I was trying to keep the heat off you if I could."

Charlie shrugged. "I'm not worried about it, neither is Liz. We did nothing wrong and everything up to this point is mere coincidence." She put the magazine down and sat up. "Plus, we know how to handle ourselves."

"Well, excuse me for trying to be thoughtful," Nora snapped. She didn't know why she was getting all worked up. It was all a lie. She hadn't been ignoring them to protect them. She'd done it to protect herself and give herself time to think. Still, in that moment, staring into Charlie's skeptic gaze, she didn't want to back down. Even if it meant she told another lie. What was one more at this point?

"Okay, you two, that's enough," Liz said, speaking up for the first time. "Thanks for watching out for us, even if *one of us* is a bit paranoid."

Nora decided to back off. She hadn't come here to argue. She'd come to get answers. Not to mention, she did miss her friends. "How have you guys been?"

"Fine," Liv answered. "It's been quiet at home. My uncle's been out gathering evidence and trying to help with Kyle's case. He does a lot of the grunt work." The way Liv said it, Nora knew she was embarrassed. She was so tired of this invisible line she could still feel between them.

"Hey, did you know that this morning was the first time I've had breakfast with my dad in more than five years. And he was actually smiling and talking, not barking demanding questions."

"What's your point?" Charlie asked.

"My point is, life isn't perfect, no matter how good it looks. My dad may have a good job, but my mom doesn't have one at all. We may have money, but we've been missing joy for a long time. There's always give and take."

Liv smiled at her, a new-found appreciation sparked in her eyes. "Truth."

After that, the girls chatted about home life. The barrier Nora broke opened a door she was happy to walk right through. Charlie had three brothers, who, from the sound of it, seemed to be a handful. Their mother could barely handle them when their father was gone. Charlie's dad was a contractor who traveled a lot to support all six of them.

Liv's mom had died six years ago in a car crash out west while away on business. Her dad bailed shortly after that, leaving Liv with her mom's sister. Liv loved her aunt and uncle, but often wondered about her dad. Her goal was to one day work her way up into the police department, find her dad, and demand to know why he left her. She understood him having a broken heart, but hadn't leaving his daughter been just as hard? Nora didn't have answers for her, but she vowed to one day help her find them.

Nora told them about her workaholic dad and depressed mom. She told them about how it had once been and then one day, it was all different. Her dad had received a new position in the firm and it became priority number one. She didn't mention anything about Beth. She was glad her and the girls were talking on a more personal level now, but Beth's secret was going to have to wait for another day.

Nora checked her watch once she'd gotten her sob story out. She was going to have to leave soon in order to get home in time for dinner. "I don't mean to shift gears here, but I'm going to have to scoot soon. What's this theory you have?" Nora asked, directing the question to Charlie.

Charlie glanced at Liv who gave her a nod of encouragement. Charlie winced. "You're not going to like it," she said.

"Try me," Nora challenged.

Charlie took a deep breath. "I think it's Gary." When Nora's expression remained blank, Charlie went on to emphasize for her. "The president of the debate team, Gary."

A laugh escaped Nora. "Gary, as in freaking-the-hell-out-and-needing-my-inhaler Gary?" If there was one thing she couldn't imagine, it was Gary murdering someone, especially someone like Kyle. "Have you ever met Gary? He doesn't have a backbone at all."

"I know it sounds crazy but hear me out." Charlie sat with the same air she did when presenting her case during their meets. This time, though, it was real and she was putting on her best show. "His aunt was at the library on four different occasions while we were here."

"His aunt?" Nora asked, not getting how this could possibly relate. Or aware of the fact that Gary had an aunt. She'd met his grandparents, parents, and uncle. He'd never mentioned an aunt, not that they were besties, but he talked about his family a lot. They were all successful and he wanted everyone to know about it. Not once did he mention an aunt. Not that Nora could remember anyway.

"Yeah. Turns out she married someone they didn't approve of from another state. She was pushed to the sidelines, basically. She lives in Angel Grove."

Nora snorted. It wasn't like Angel Grove was some disregarded neighborhood. It was beautiful with immaculate houses, trimmed hedges, and nice gardens. It was also a step down from Pinewood Estates, which was where the rest of Gary's family lived.

"The family still gets together, including his Aunt Sarah. After some Instagram stalking, I found a few posts of her with her family. Not as many as her parents have with their son, but a few. This past Sunday they all had dinner at Gary's grandparents' house. It would have been easy for her to bring it up in conversation."

"How does something like that even come up in conversation?" Nora asked. How did one casually bring up seeing someone they didn't know?

"Easy. 'Hey, Gary, I saw your debate friend at the library today. Sweet girl.' That simple," Charlie answered.

Nora flushed. She hated small talk, therefore she didn't understand it. "Where are you getting all your information?"

"I hacked the system. Duh." Yes, because that was a normal everyday task. "I did a background check on all the people who were at the library thirty minutes before, during, and after our meetings. She was the most consistent."

It was a reasonable idea. If Gary's aunt had seen them, maybe even heard what they were discussing, and mentioned it to Gary, he could have easily come to the library and spied on them to see what was going on. The problem Nora had with him being Charlie's suspect was motive. "It makes sense, but it doesn't make sense. Why would Gary kill Kyle?"

"To get rid of the competition," she said, as if it was the most obvious thing ever, but Charlie and Liv didn't know the ins and outs of the debate team. They didn't know that Nora was no competition to Gary.

"Gary has no competition. None. He is the president, as in voted in by the group. There's no one above him, and considering he's a senior like me, he has no reason to fight for a position next year." Nora hadn't been surprised Gary had been voted in as president; she'd voted for him herself. It was when she'd won vice president that she'd been surprised. She was smart enough for the position. It was the social aspect of it. She'd often wondered if Gary had something to do with her getting a position on the team. He was strategic about everything and knew they were the strongest in the group. He'd have no reason to set Nora up for murder. If he wanted to get rid of her, he had the power to do it.

Nora went on to explain all of that to Liv and Charlie. "See," she said once she was finished, "he has no reason to set me up for murder. He has the power to get rid of me by vetoing me out if he wanted."

"Would he do it for attention?" Charlie asked. "Would any of them do it for attention?"

Anger flooded through Nora. "Why, because we are a bunch of bored, spoiled rich kids?" Sure, Charlie had done good research on the patrons who had visited the library during their meetings. She'd done her job in connecting them with people they interacted with. Where she'd failed was gathering a motive, and now it felt as if she was trying to push an idea rather than having proof.

Charlie cursed in her native Spanish tongue and then swiveled on Liv. "I told you she wouldn't believe it was one of her own."

"And I told you not to say it like that," Liv snapped. "We're her *friends*, Charlie. We don't say things like 'one of her own'."

Nora gathered up her things and slung her backpack onto her shoulder. "No need for that, Liv. I'm glad to know where I stand to you two."

Liv called out after Nora as she rushed past the circulation desk. Nora ignored her. Anger burned through her, as did hurt. The hurt settled in deep and clenched tightly at her chest with every step she took home.

Chapter Ten

It was Friday night and Nora was doing what she did every Friday night, holed up in her room with a book and Netflix on the ready. She liked the quiet pace staying in offered her. Plus, she never got invited to go anywhere. On occasion, when her sister was up to it, the two of them would go to the movies. The one and only time since Beth's incident that she'd been invited out by two girls on the debate team, she'd smiled and laughed at all the right moments, but apparently, she hadn't contributed much for another invite.

With a sigh of aggravation, she set her book down on the nightstand and stared up at the ceiling. She'd been waiting for this particular book to be released, even counted down the days. Now, she could care less. Her heart wasn't into it. Her mind was on what Charlie had said to her yesterday. On how she accused Gary of being the murderer, although there was no true reason for him to try and frame Nora.

It wasn't that she hadn't given it more thought, she had. Was there a reason for Gary to want Nora out of the picture? He was the president of the debate team, had scored a point higher on the SATs, and was valedictorian of their class. He had no reason to want to take her out of the picture. As for colleges, he had his sites on Harvard. Nora was looking farther west.

She'd considered the romantic aspect. She'd read many cases of murderers killing their lovers for unusual reasons and jealousy. The thought had made her laugh as she sat in English class writing out positive and negative responses for Gary being the killer. Gary having a crush on her, ha. Thinking of the disgusted snarl he'd given her for missing the other day, she was sure that wasn't the case. She didn't know much about love or crushes, but treating the other person as if they repulsed you wasn't how it was done.

Groaning, she rolled over onto her stomach and started cruising through Netflix. She wasn't going to be able to concentrate on the words that would eventually carry her away into the story. She was too wrapped up in her own story.

After fifteen minutes of unappealing television surfing, Nora turned off the large flat screen tv. No matter what she tried doing, her thoughts were surrounded by the what ifs and uncertainty of the future. The loneliness of it all was the worst. Her friendship with Liv and Charlie had been nothing to them. She was just another freak, fascinated by the mystery behind murder like they were, who was lonely enough to bring their online club to life.

Liv had texted her three times last night claiming Charlie didn't mean what she said. They were her friends. She wasn't alone in this. Blah, blah, blah. Nora hadn't bothered to text her back. It wasn't out of spite. It was because she didn't know what to make of Charlie's accusations. She didn't know what to make of her friendship with the two girls, either. She was fed up with lying and didn't have it in her to pretend it was okay. It wasn't okay, so she'd left it alone.

Biting her lip and staring at her phone, Nora thought about Reed. He hadn't been at school for two days. It'd been fifty-six hours since he'd given her his number. Fifty-six hours of back and forth as to whether she should text him or not, and if she did, what would she say? This was her break. Her open door into conversation.

Nora: Hey, Reed. It's Nora. Everything okay? Noticed you've been MIA.

After hitting send, she stared at her phone with anticipation while chastising every word she sent. She tried occupying her mind and pretending she wasn't on edge waiting for his reply by dragging out her book again. It was a nice lie to tell herself. It sure made her feel better and less mental. When her phone did ding minutes later, she swore her heart skipped a few beats.

Reed: Been out sick. Nasty cold.

She stared at the screen, not knowing what to say. She wanted to say something to keep the conversation going. She hadn't texted him for a quick 'how are you' 'fine' exchange. She'd wanted to talk and get to know him. She'd wanted to get her mind off everything going on, if only for a little while. Texting 'that sucks' would end all conversation and she knew it. Lucky for her she didn't have to worry about it.

Reed: Mind if I call you? I hate texting.

Relief eased the weight on her mind as she texted him back.

Nora: Sure!

Normally she'd prefer texting, but this was uncharted territory and sometimes talking helped guide her social queues. It wasn't ten seconds after she hit send that her phone buzzed in her hand. She let it ring twice before answering. The last thing she wanted to do was appear desperate.

"Hello," she answered.

"Hey, sorry about that. I know I'm out of the circle with the texting craze, but I honestly hate it."

Nora smiled. It was silly to admire someone for something so simple, but she did. She'd bet money eighty percent of her classmates couldn't function right without being able to text. "If you don't mind me asking, why? What about it do you hate?"

"Too much waiting, not to mention it's a complete waste of time. Why would you not want to laugh with the person you're speaking with rather than send one of those ridiculous emojis to let them know you're laughing. Of course, I'm being raised by my grandparents so I could have them to blame for brainwashing me. If you ever meet them, never say 'apps' in front of them."

She laughed, liking his logic. Reed chuckled too. "See, laughter together, it's much better."

"I want to ask why they hate apps, but I have a feeling it's due to being forced to accept an app over good ole fashioned paperwork." She'd heard her own grandfather complaining about the same thing one day after going to the doctor. He had a smartphone, so downloading the app hadn't been that big of a chore for him. However, he had grumbled about having to check in and fill out his information on the app while waiting in the lobby. Turned out, the receptionist had to double check with him that all his information was correct once he was done. She could still hear him now. *If she was going to have to go through it anyway, why didn't she just do it to begin with? It seems like we are doubling our work input into these apps for the sake of technological convenience.*

"That's it. Something to do with their prescriptions and digital coupons, I don't know. They grumble about it all." His voice sounded lazy, like he was fighting sleep.

"You sound tired. Do you need to go?" Nora wasn't ready to hang up, but she didn't want to be a nuisance either. When she was sick, she wanted zero communication with anyone.

He yawned. "No. I don't want to sleep. Tell me something," he prompted. "Make it interesting."

She couldn't help but laugh. "What makes you think anything I have to say is interesting?" Her stomach twisted. She had some interesting news, but there was no way she could tell him about it. He'd think she was crazy.

"I don't know, but something tells me there's a few secrets buried deep inside of you that make what you perceive as ordinary extraordinary."

Heat rose up Nora's neck and spread across her cheeks. "Maybe, but don't we all?"

Another chuckle filtered through the phone. She was starting to like the sound of him being amused. "Well, I can see this is going to go nowhere if I don't kick us off."

"Whoa, philosophy and then a football simile. You're all over the charts."

"Like I said, a few secrets." She could imagine the smile on his face. The crinkle to his eyes. Doubt tried creeping into her mind, but she shoved it aside. It wasn't like he was asking her for world secrets or anything. It was friendly conversation. Yes, it was sudden and oddly timed, but wasn't that how life rolled sometimes? "Here's a secret I bet you didn't know about me. My parents are both in the Army and are enlisted together. They are the reason I got the scholarship to Pinewood."

"That also explains why you live with your grandparents," Nora added. She had taken note of his admission earlier but didn't want to pry. She'd told herself if he wanted her to know he would tell her, just like Liv and Charlie had. She was glad to hear his parents hadn't died or skipped town.

"Yeah. They're both Army brats who couldn't break out of the mold. After serving a tour, they met at a base in Belgium. It was insta-love from what I understand. Dad's served for twenty-one years, Mom for nineteen. If you count the two years she took off to birth me and spend a little time raising me before going MIA, then it's seventeen years." The bitterness was heavy and solid. "I shouldn't be so bitter, I know. They're doing a good service."

"Fun fact, did you know by doing a good service we often do a bad service at the same time. It's this balancing act called life." And Beth thought all those philosophy and psychology books were crap. Nora lived and breathed by them.

"I don't buy that," Reed replied, a fire now in his tone. Nora could feel the debate rising and she was ready.

"Why not? It makes perfect sense. Life is give and take, therefore when we put in something there's a give and something is taken out." Nora knew she was misquoting her philosophy teacher she had last summer but she remembered the gist of it.

"That's insane. Okay, so, if I was to give a homeless man on the street a muffin, what's the bad side of that?"

Nora liked the challenge in his voice. "Depends on the circumstances. Was this muffin your breakfast and you had no more money to buy something else, therefore causing hunger and delaying your brain's response time? Did it have a substance that had been recalled due to salmonella poisoning or E. coli? Was the man allergic to any of the ingredients? There has to be a scene setting."

"Dang, got to be technical?" he laughed. He was silent for a few minutes, probably thinking over how to move forward with the argument. Nora smiled. She liked making people sweat. "Okay, let's say none of that. I was heading home from work. I had more food at home. I'd bought the muffin for a snack, but it wasn't something I had to have. There was no salmonella or E. coli. He wasn't allergic. What then? Normal, beautiful day. Guy walking down the street and hands another less fortunate guy a muffin and skips along without incident."

"The homeless man chokes on a bread crumb that goes down the wrong way. A man stops to help him. Is late for a meeting for the third time that month and is fired. Bam. Good and bad."

"Wow. That's some imagination you have there. What's wrong with thinking the guy walked away and the homeless man was satisfied and had a smile on his face?" The way Reed said it didn't make Nora feel like a freak. She felt like he understood but wanted to hear her reasoning.

For the first time, she had none. "There's nothing wrong with it," she said with a smile. "It's perfect." The philosophy went against what she was taught, but Nora was starting to realize not everything she was ever told and taught was right. Sometimes, people learn to make their own rules of life.

"Wow. I never thought I would get you to give in like that. I've seen you compete. You're pretty fierce."

That took Nora by surprise. "You've seen me compete? When?"

"A couple months ago. Kyle wanted to go. He had some elaborate plan to embarrass Gary for the dick move he'd pulled. Good thing for Gary, Kyle never showed. I stayed for a while before bailing in round three."

"It can get pretty intense," she said, nervous. She'd never known someone other than her family, who rarely went to her debates, was watching her. It was probably a good thing she hadn't known.

"All right, I've spilled something interesting," he said. "Now, it's your turn."

Nora stared up at the ceiling, her heart hammering away. She wanted to talk to someone about what was happening with the flyers and Kyle and how it all could come back on her. It was driving her mad that she was keeping it all bottled up to herself. Plus, she could use some advice with handling the police. Should she tell them what she knew or not?

The words were on the tip of her tongue, but yet, she held them back. Reed was new territory that she hadn't figured out yet. She wanted to know that he could handle how crazy her theories were without flaking out on her. "Honestly, there's nothing interesting about me."

"I doubt that," he mused. "Let me ask you a question then. I'll warn you, it's personal and if you don't want to talk about it, it's fine." He was calm, which set Nora at ease. As did the reassurance that she didn't have to talk about it. "Ever since the flyer came out Tuesday there's been a lot of chatter about you." Nora's stomach dropped. She had a feeling she knew where this was going. "Something about you being like your sister."

He didn't ask a specific question, but she knew what he was hinting at. What happened with Beth to make people say something like that about Nora? She rolled over onto her side and stared at the picture she kept on her bedside table. It was of her and Beth, not long before Beth's incident. They were bundled up with snow covering every inch of their clothing. Laughter filled the still moment as neither one of them looked at the camera.

"Nora, you still there?" Reed asked, his voice soft and comforting.

She closed her eyes. "Yes."

"Like I said, you don't have to talk about it. I was just curious."

She sighed. It was a start to talking to him, and since everyone else knew, why not clue him in? "Beth had a mental breakdown three years ago. It happened at a birthday party she didn't even want to go to. It was my fault. I was the one who pushed her." Tears scorched at Nora's eyes as she pictured that day all over again. "I'd been so terrible to her. She'd been having some issues at school, you know. Feeling left out and like she didn't fit in. The normal middle school drama. I told her going to the party would be good for her, that it would help ease her mind. When she kept insisting she didn't want to go..." Nora's throat closed off and she had to clear her it. "I called her so many lousy names. Told her she was crazy and would end up being the loner she feared she was if she didn't step up. Fake it until you make it, right?" A sour laugh ripped through her tear-clogged chest. "It was shitty, real shitty."

"What happened at the party?" Reed asked.

Nora thought back to that frantic phone call from Macy White's mom. "Beth went and she tried, God, I know she tried, but she panicked. She was freaking out and the other girls started making fun of her. They were pushing her around and poking fun at her, which only made it worse. Beth snapped. She started throwing things and hitting the girls. She pushed one girl so hard she broke her arm and another girl came away with a black eye. She just... lost it."

"Sounds like they had it coming."

Nora had thought the same thing but had never voiced it. Her mother was a frantic mess when they arrived at the White's house. Nora had walked in to find Beth sitting alone in the sitting room, her face streaked with tears. She listened to her mother apologize over and over to Mrs. White while Mr. White escorted the girls home. All the while she held Beth and glared at each one as they passed by. "Twenty-four hours later Beth was seeing the best child psychologist in the area and was diagnosed with bipolar depression and anxiety."

"Dang. And it was all because of a birthday party?"

"No. Dr. Woods said it was due to too much at one time. Our brains can only process and handle so much, some more some less. Beth had too much happening in a short period of time, meaning weeks, and her brain couldn't handle it. Her body snapped and went into flight mode to survive." She thought about his family admission earlier and decided to give in a little. She wanted to show him a level of trust. "We had our own family issues happening too."

Reed snorted. "Don't we all on some level?"

For the next two hours they talked about everything and nothing at all. They covered favorite movies. His was

Twister because of the action and appeal of tornadoes since they didn't get them that often in New York. Nora's was *Practical Magic*. What she wouldn't do to be an Owens girl. After talking favorite color and what made it so appealing, Nora stretched out on her bed and glanced at the clock.

"Wow. I don't think I have ever talked on the phone this long." She couldn't believe it was after midnight. She'd never talked on the phone this long. Record!

Reed yawned. "Yeah, me either."

"Thanks for talking with me tonight. I really needed a laugh." Her face warmed at the admission.

"Happy to help," he said with amusement in his tone. "And Nora, what happened with Beth wasn't your fault. No one could have predicted she would have a fall out like that. For all we know, some guy down the street gave a homeless man a muffin and sent bad juju her way."

Laughter filled her room. "You're crazy."

"Not as much as you."

She was about to say goodnight and tell him she'd see him on Monday when her bedroom door flew open and Beth came running into her room. "You're not going to believe this. Look at this." Beth held out her phone for Nora to see.

Beth's Instagram page was pulled up, and in the center of the screen was the Channel 5 News logo. The heading: *Boy Found In Alley, Multiple Burn Marks*. The words began to blur as she read the words over and over again. "It can't be," she whispered. *Liv!*

"Nora?" Reed's worried voice snapped her back to the moment. "Nora, what's wrong?"

"They found another body," she whispered, the possibilities and shock still slogging her thoughts. "What have I done?" The words were a whisper, only a thought for herself, but she'd said them before hitting that blessed red button.

Chapter Eleven

The air felt stale, as if life hadn't been breathed into the house all night. Nora knew it was her paranoid imagination. She'd been up all night breathing, though it felt forced at times. How could another person be dead? It was an all-time crime break for Lake Placid. The question she couldn't put in her puzzle was why.

Her feet felt heavy as she descended the stairs and made her way into the kitchen, where the smell of fresh coffee was strong in the air. Her mom sat at the table, coffee mug in one hand, tablet in the other. She'd expected to find her mother in the same position she was after discovering the news about Kyle: hunched in front of the television, sad look on her face, sympathetic words filling the air every three seconds. Instead, her mom looked more chipper than ever.

"Good morning, honey. Did you sleep well?"

Nora skipped over the pleasantries. "Have you heard the news?"

Her mom's brow furrowed. "What news? Is everything okay?"

"They found another body. This one was on the west side of town." The coffee mugs clanked together as Nora pulled out a mug. They had enough coffee mugs to invite the whole neighborhood over.

Her mother sighed. "I did hear about that. It's terrible." She picked up her tablet. "Did you see the flyers? I'm sure Amy Hollis will be over any minute to cry about it."

Nora's stomach turned. What had happened between six and eight? "What flyers?" she managed to ask while fighting back the fear building in her.

"The flyers. The ones they posted last time about the debate team." Seeing Nora's blank face, which was really a mask of the horror she felt inside, her mom picked up her tablet and held it up. There was a picture of a telephone pole with a white piece of paper stapled to it. Nora stepped closer so she could read what it said.

Two down, how many more to go? The debate is on.

Below the cryptic message was a gavel like last time. In the background, question marks floated in all shapes and sizes. Nora grabbed the counter, unsure if she was going to pass out or throw up.

"Honey, are you okay?" her mother asked as she stood up from the table.

"I just need a minute." Lifting her arms above her head, she took deep, solid breaths. She could not break down, not now. There's was too much at stake for her to clock out now. "Can I borrow your car?" It was a stupid question to ask in the condition she was in, but Nora was desperate. She really didn't feel like walking today, not after the long night she had. She would if it came to it, but she was going to take her chances first.

"Where, might I ask, do you think you're capable of driving in this condition?" Her mother's worried eyes searched her face.

It was now or never, truth or lie. "I need to go see a friend and make sure she's okay."

"Who is this friend?" Her mother's eyes slit with suspicion.

"She's from West High. I'm pretty sure she knew the guy that was killed." Nora kept her back straight, her eyes focused on her mom. Something flickered there, understanding or maybe pride, Nora wasn't sure, but the look of disappointment she thought she was going to see wasn't there.

"You know, you didn't have to keep your friends hidden from us." Confusion crossed Nora's face and her mother rolled her eyes. "Did you honestly think I wouldn't find out from Mrs. Nosey Noose? She called me not five minutes after she dropped off Kenzie to tell me you were walking with two strange girls down the street. I then added that I saw you walking with the two girls and that it was okay. She didn't seem to like that at all."

If there was ever a moment – besides the time they had walked into Mrs. White's home to get Beth – that Nora had felt like an ass, this was it. "I just thought…." She trailed off, not wanting to say the rest of it and hating herself for even having the words inside of her.

"I know what you thought. You thought we wouldn't approve." Her mom placed both hands on her shoulders and pulled her closer. "That's my fault. I have my own issues to deal with. As long as you're happy, safe, and still have your own goals, I'm good and so is your father." She took a deep breath and then leaned her forehead against Nora's. "We all have some growing to do, baby girl. Even though I'm an adult, I've got a way to go. I've made mistakes when it's come to you girls and your father. All we can do is learn and move forward. I hate that it took a tragedy to snap us out of it, but no matter, we're here and we have to face it."

"Does this mean no more community luncheons at our house?"

Her mom laughed. "Baby steps. Besides, you know what they say, keep your friends close but your enemies closer."

Nora didn't know why but the statement made her cringe. Was her enemy close and she hadn't realized it? She had gone over all the possibilities of who was at the library when the group met and if they had any connections with the girls. But what if it wasn't someone who was at the library? What if it was someone else who had been close, yet distant?

"Nora, are you okay?" her mother asked as she peered down at her with concern.

"Yeah, just tired and a little worried. You mind about the car?"

"I don't mind, but I do have one rule. You have to be back home before dark." Nora opened her mouth to protest but her mother cut her off. "This is nonnegotiable. I don't mind you going to see your friends, but there are people out there who would see a car like mine and tear it to shreds, or better yet, steal it with you inside. Home before dark."

Thirty minutes later, with her lip raw from chewing on it, she pulled to the front of Liv's house. It was a quaint house with red bricks and white trimmings. The walk was framed by rocks and landscape timbers. A bird bath sat in the center of the yard, with concrete frogs and butterflies scaling its sides up to the lily pad that held water for the birds.

As she was getting out of the car, her phone dinged.

Reed: You okay?

She hit ignore and opted to leave her phone in the car. Charlie wasn't texting her. Beth was being clingy and wanting to know why she couldn't go with her, to which she had no answer that didn't sound rude. And Reed, well, she didn't know what to say to him. In her moment of shock last night, she distinctively remembered saying, "What have I done?" before hanging up the phone. She was sure he was wanting some answers as to what she meant. She didn't have any for him.

After knocking on the door, she shoved her hands in her pocket and rocked back and forth on her heels. She didn't know what she was going to say, but she needed to be here. Liv and Charlie had come for her after Kyle's death. It was only right that she paid them the same respect, even though she'd been a crappy friend the last few days.

A man wearing a LPPD hoodie and sweat pants opened the door. "You're not Maco," he greeted with a smile. "You're much prettier."

"Oh God," Liv said, pushing around the man. "Never mind my uncle. He can be a little weird. Maco is his running buddy, btw."

Nora smiled up at the man as Liv dragged her by the arm past him.

"Name's James," he called after them.

"Nora," she yelled back over her shoulder before being pulled into a room and the door slammed shut between them. The first thing Nora noticed about the room was how homey it felt. The light was dimmed and gave off a soft glow against the cream-colored walls. White light strands with pictures clipped between each bulb lined the ceiling. In the corner was a day bed with enough pillows to make another bed on the floor. A small desk stacked with books sat in the corner. To her left, a closet was overflowing with clothes into the room.

"Don't judge," Liv warned as she flopped down onto the bed. "I know it's not as nice as your place, but it's home. My home."

It was funny how off Liv was. "You're wrong. It's better than nice. It's cozy."

"Yeah, that sounds way better," Liv remarked, her tone dripping with sarcasm.

"Trust me," Nora said as she wiggled in next to Liv. "It is."

"You're telling me your room isn't cozy?" Liv asked, calling a bluff that wasn't there.

"Think about it. Big means spacious. Alone in a spacious room isn't always comforting." She started laughing when she thought about her room. "You need to come over to my house to see for yourself. Most of my things are pushed into one corner. The bed is in the center and everything else in the right corner. The rest is bare and left open."

"All the more room for dancing," Liv stated.

That was a scary idea. "Trust me, you don't not want to see this dancing. It's like trying to watch a deer walk on ice."

Liv laughed as she rested her arm over her forehead. "This is a mess." It was a simple statement in the grand scheme of things.

"It is. Did you notice that it?"

"Followed my scenario from a couple of weeks ago? I did. Did you know it was Charlie's older brother's best friend Ryan?"

Nora blanched. "Charlie knew him?"

"Had dinner with him last night. He lived next door." Liv bit her lip and looked at Nora with a sidelong look. Tears brimmed her eyes. "This is too much. Why would someone do this? Who is doing it?"

Nora crossed her arms over her chest and stared up at the ceiling. She felt like she was about to come undone. "I don't know. I've been up all night thinking about what Charlie said, about Gary, but this doesn't fit. Why would he attack someone from West? There's no connection."

Liv shifted, her arm covering her face once again. "I was thinking the same. But if not him, then who?"

"I don't know, but maybe we should go to the police. They could help us." It had been a crazy idea at first, admitting to the police that they had created the scenes and that it had all been for fun. To Nora, and what she knew from studying criminal investigation, they'd become prime suspects. But now, with another death on the list, she wasn't so sure.

Liv shuddered beside her. "I wish we could, but we can't. Trust me, we would be under the radar as suspects, not as witnesses. There would be no sympathy, at all." She picked at the fabric of her wool sweater with her other hand. "I talked to my uncle, gave him a scenario similar to ours. He said they'd be prime suspects as they knew every detail. The police wouldn't trust them until they cleared them or caught the real killer."

Nora let her hand fall off the side of the bed. It dangled, just like her thoughts. As she stared up at the lights she thought back to the days of her life, not so long ago, that were simple. Days where she dreamed of being a part of the mystery. Now that she was neck deep in being framed for murder, she wasn't sure she was cut out for it.

"You know, she won't even talk to me," Liv whispered, still picking at her shirt.

"Who?" Nora asked, although she had a feeling she knew who by the deep sadness in Liv's tone.

"Charlie. She said she couldn't trust anyone right now."

Nora startled, not expecting that. Liv and Charlie were best friends. "That's insane. If there's one person on the planet she can trust, it's you."

"You know," Liv said, turning to look at her, "I thought that too. That is until she proved me wrong."

Nora's heart wrenched for Liv as a tear slid down her face. "Hey, don't take it to heart. She's hurting. People say awful things when they are hurting and confused." She thought back to a fight her and Beth had a few weeks back. "You know, my sister has bipolar depression so sometimes it's hard feeling out her true emotions. I struggled with it, still do sometimes, because it hurts. She can act so self-centered and hateful. Say the most horrible things, especially when you push her and she doesn't feel like being pushed. But then, when the storm calms down and she remembers what she said, she always apologizes and tells me she didn't mean it. I knew she didn't mean it, but the apology means something, especially when you know they are just trying to handle the life they've been dealt. Is it fair? No. It's not fair that they can say those things and we later forgive them. But there's also a line of understanding, of watching them try, that needs to be understood."

Disbelief clouded Liv's gaze. Nora understood. When the therapist had told her pretty much the same thing, she almost threw a book at him. "So, what? I should go running to Charlie like nothing was said."

"No," Nora said, stern. "You let her come to you. Give her time to think, process, and realize what she did. Then you will know the apology is real."

"How do you deal with that so much?" Liv asked.

Nora stared up at the ceiling, picturing Beth's smiling face. "Because I see her trying."

Chapter Twelve

Liv and Nora made plans to meet up at the library Monday after school. They had to figure out who was behind all of this. The days of sitting around waiting for the next punch in the gut were over. It was time to figure out the real murderer, not figuring one out from a line off an index card. Nora had wanted to go right away, but Liv wasn't up to it. She gave a lame remark saying the library would be closing soon since it was Saturday and that it wasn't worth it. Nora thought otherwise.

After telling Liv not to forget what she said about forgiving Charlie, Nora left and headed for downtown. Her brain was on fire as thought after thought processed through her mind. She wished Liv or Beth or maybe even Reed was there with her, helping her process her thoughts. She hated being at it alone. Thinking of Reed made her think of his text message earlier. Picking up her phone, she saw she had one missed call and three text messages from Beth and one more from Reed. She skipped past Beth's to read his.

Reed: What's going on? Don't hide from me. Please.

Her heart sank. It wasn't that she was hiding. It was that she was afraid. As much as she loved Beth, she didn't want to be labeled. The reality was, she was afraid Reed would label her as crazy. That she didn't know if she could handle. This, figuring out who was the mastermind behind all these schemes, she could handle. She hoped.

A red light stopped Nora in the street, a block from the library. "Okay," she breathed. "Focus." She'd tell Reed if it came to it, but that day was not today. Today was a day for figuring out the truth. The sooner Nora did that, the sooner everyone's lives could go back to normal.

As she pulled into the parking lot, she gathered her thoughts and started processing her questions. She was going to have to be tactical. Odd-ball questions would get her looked at. Prying questions would alert alarm. Casual, she needed to be casual. She loosened the scarf around her neck and peered at herself in the mirror. As she was fixing her lip gloss, she rolled her eyes at herself. "What are you doing? It's a library not a first date." Tossing the lip gloss to the side, she got out and faced the bitter New York air. The wind was howling and she had to wrap the scarf back around her neck to keep the snow from flying down her shirt.

She struggled with the door but managed to pull its metal frame against the power of the wind. When she stumbled inside, a man standing next to the magazine rack chuckled. "It's a windy one today."

She resisted the "Gee, ya think" that was on the tip of her tongue and turned to the desk clerk. Luckily, there were only two that worked the desk on a regular basis and they both happened to be working.

"Hey, ladies," she said in her best Girl Scout's volume. "How are you today?"

The woman sitting fluffed at her curls while squinting at a computer screen. Nora caught a glimpse at her name tag.

Charlotte. "Good, though it looks like a storm is brewing. It's worse than what the weather man anticipated."

The other lady, Vivian, crossed her arms and leaned forward to look at the screen. "We may need to close early."

Charlotte laughed. "Like Dave is going to let us do that. He's more worried about stats than lives." She looked up and her eyes widened. She'd forgotten Nora was standing there. A light rose color shaded her face. "I'm sorry. Did you need help with something?"

"Actually, yes. Me and my friends meet here on Thursday nights."

"Oh yes," Vivian cooed. "There are three of you."

"Yes, ma'am. Liv and Charlie. Well, Liv left her backpack here one night and it had her wallet inside. Has anyone turned it in?" Now for them to bite and not wave her off passively.

The two women looked at each other, brows pinched as they thought back to someone returning a forgotten backpack. "I don't think so," Charlotte said.

"I'll go check in the back," Vivian added. "I'm not here on Monday and Wednesday mornings. Sometimes things get past me."

"I'm here," Charlotte protested and haughtily looked up at the other woman. "I would have remembered."

"I know that," Vivian said, though she looked like she didn't. "But you could have been in the bathroom. I'll be right back. It won't take a second."

Charlotte looked miffed and glanced back at her computer screen. "She always thinks she knows everything."

Nora smiled. "Have you two worked together for a while?"

"The last thirty years. And in that thirty years, nothing has changed." She gave a bitter glance over her shoulder. "She thinks she rules the roost."

Nora smiled. Charlotte could be her winning ticket. "Thirty years, I bet you know everyone who comes in here."

"I sure do," she said with pride and pointed at the man standing at the magazine rack. "He probably does too. Mr. Rivets is in here every day reading magazines and greeting people at the door." Nora looked over at him and made note of his name. Hello, suspect number one.

Vivian came out from the office in the back with a puckered lip of apology. "I am so sorry, dear, but there was no backpack in the lost and found."

Nora closed her eyes and did her best to sell the man-that-sucks vibe. "Are there any Thursday regulars who I can reach out to and ask if they may have seen it or saw someone pick it up?" She held her breath. It was the question to top off the lead up of lies. Now, she could only hope it worked. She feared there would be some patron privacy rule.

Lucky for her, these two ladies didn't seem to mind. "Beside Mr. Rivets, no one comes to mind," Vivian said.

"That's because you're senile," Charlotte snapped. "There's Ms. Humphrey who comes on Wednesday and Thursday afternoons to do puzzles. There's Mrs. Segmeyer who carries in that crying toddler and gets her weekend fixes; baby books, dvds, a book for herself, those kinds of things. Then there's that sweet boy, what's his name," she asked looking up to Vivian, "Rev?"

Vivian snapped her fingers. "Reed." A wave of heat swept through Nora. Reed? Had he been around the whole time? Her heart raced with her thoughts as possibilities and doubt started forming in her mind. Then Vivian's face scrunched and she started shaking her head. "No, no, no. He comes on Friday's, remember. He gets a new puzzle for that grandma of his." She rolled her eyes and mumbled, "And you call me senile," as she focused back on the computer.

Nora got a few more names jotted down on her list and thanked the women for their help. Some her and Charlie had already checked into, but there were two names they hadn't. Mr. Rivets and Mrs. Colley who lived down the street from Nora. She couldn't imagine the old woman who hardly left her house trying to frame her for murder, but stranger things had happened. Maybe she had looked at the woman cross eyed one day and didn't know it. Either way, she was going to check into it. Maybe she had a grandkid in Nora's class.

While she was there, Nora walked back to the nonfiction section. The library was closing in twenty minutes, but she had time to browse the true crime section. She glanced out the window as she passed the side entrance. Snow was beginning to fall as the wind gusted and blew it in angry waves through the streets. If she didn't leave soon, she may not be able to get home. She could think of worse places to get stuck; the library wasn't one of them.

She'd just turned the corner in the third row of stacks when she slammed into someone coming around the bend. Books fell to the floor and she bent over to pick them up as she muttered an apology. One of the titles caught her attention: *Criminal Profiling: An Introductory Guide.* Her focus was on the book as she stood back up.

"I've read this one," she said, still not looking at the person. "It's really informative." She then looked up and her eyes went wide. "Reed?"

He took the book from her. "Thanks," he said and tucked the book into the crook of his arm. "Surprised to see you here."

The remark took her off guard. "Why? Because it's a public library?"

He rolled his eyes. "No. Because you haven't been answering my texts, so I thought you were sick or something."

Nora's stomach burned. She hated facing confrontations, especially when she was the cause of them. "I'm sorry," she muttered. "I went to see a friend this morning and I've been a little wrapped up."

"This friend have anything to do with the kid who was killed yesterday?" The bluntness of his tone shook her. Was he starting to catch on to her?

"Yes," she said, figuring the truth was better right now. What was the point in lying? "It was her brother's best friend."

"You know Charlie?" he asked. She'd forgot he lived on the west side of town. He probably knew most of the kids that went to West.

Nora pushed her hands into her coat pocket, trying to protect herself from the slew of questions that were probably about to be thrown her way. Glancing at the book, she decided to try and divert. "What are you doing reading criminal profiling?"

Reed rubbed the back of his head, embarrassment crossing his face. "I don't know, researching?"

"Researching what?" she pushed.

Indecision clouded his eyes as he peered down at her. Was he sizing her up? Did he suspect her of something? Hurt registered in her chest as he peered around and seemed to make a snap decision. Grabbing her by the elbow, he pulled her back down the aisle and out of view. "Listen, I don't know what's going on and I wish you would tell me, because I know you know something."

Her flight instincts pulled at her and she started to pull out of his grip when he lightly gave her arm a squeeze. "You can trust me, Nora. I swear." When she still didn't say anything and doubt was all that shown on her face, he pushed forward. "Last night you said, 'What have I done?'. I know you're not a murderer." He held up his hand when she opened her mouth to question him. "Call it a gut instinct," he said, answering her questioning look. "But I want to help. I don't know what you've gotten yourself into, but someone is trying to make a point. It has to stop." He pulled away and straightened, sadness deep in his eyes. "I can't take losing anyone else I know."

The hurt in his voice made Nora hurt for him. "You knew Ryan?"

Reed nodded. "Grew up right beside him. He was my friend, Nora. On some level so was Kyle." He shifted the books from one arm to the other. "There. I've shared my interesting. Now it's your turn."

Nora dropped her gaze to the floor. Fear gripped at her chest. She felt like she was suffocating. "I can't."

"Why not?" he asked, his whisper a plea for a real answer.

"Because I don't want to be crazy." Tears breamed in her eyes and it was then that she realized what a hypocrite she was. She was a liar, a fake. All that sisterly love she'd told Liv about her and Beth. All the lies she'd told herself about not wanting to involve Beth because it would worry her. All the times she told herself she didn't want to tell Reed because he wouldn't understand. It was all bullshit. She hadn't told anyone, hadn't entrusted the people around her, because she was afraid she'd get that title. She would get that label. The same one Beth sported. She didn't want to live a life being looked at the way Beth was looked at, as someone you had to watch, as someone you had to half believe. And if Beth believed her, if Reed called her crazy, then she was there, knocking on the therapist's door asking to be labeled. She hated it for her sister, the bullshit she had to deal with everyday for something that was out of her control, but she also feared it for herself. She was a damn liar, always had been.

A sob ripped from her chest and she turned away from Reed, walking as fast as she could out the door. She wanted to run to escape the embarrassment and the truth that was banging at her chest. Reed called after her, but she ignored his pleas. How could she be so stupid? How could she be so shallow? People were getting murdered, her sister was a daily target for ridicule, and all she could think about was how she would look in the eyes of the world around her.

Her eyes stung from the tears swelling in their depths and the wind that whipped her hair around her face. Her hands shook as she pulled out her keys and started the car. Reed came running out of the library, his hands shielding his face against the onslaught from the wind. Nora looked away from him, ashamed. She was ashamed of the black thoughts swirling in her mind.

When Beth had first been diagnosed with bipolar depression and anxiety, Nora had felt the fear gnawing in her gut. The questions that had spiraled in her mind. Was it hereditary? Was she going to have a freak out in public one day? What were the symptoms? She had spent that whole summer researching everything she could about it and taken note of what to watch for. When school started back, she'd shoved it all down deep inside of her like a pill. She'd absorbed what she'd learnt and kept it at the forefront of her mind. First key, don't hold onto fear. So, she pushed her fear of being like her sister down the deepest, suppressing it. Instead, she focused on acting perfect. She had to prove that there was nothing wrong with her. No one asked her to prove it, but she felt the eyes on her. She felt the pressure. Until this moment, she'd done exactly what she had trained herself to do. *Put up the front, be perfect, don't draw attention to yourself, and you won't break.*

But she could feel herself breaking. Soon, everyone else would see it too. The one secret she had kept for herself, the one that didn't seem so normal in the grand scheme of life, was going to be her breaking point. What normal person was fascinated by murder and depths in which the person behind the scenes was pushed to act on such a crime? Crazy people, that was who.

Her phone dinged and she looked over at where it laid on the passenger seat. The roads were horrible, the snow so thick she could barely make out the lines. A smile crept across her face as she thought about the day her dad had first taught her how to drive in the snow.

"Keep your focus on the white and yellow lines. Don't veer too close to the white line or you'll end up sliding into the grass and getting stuck."

Beth had laughed. "In other words, keep it between the mayonnaise and mustard. Forget the lettuce unless you want your lunch lodged."

"Beth Ann," her dad had chastised, but a smile crept across his face.

All the way home she focused on the mustard, unable to see the white. When she made it safely into their driveway and put the car in park, her eyes began to sting again.

Standing in her window waiting on her to get home safely was Beth. The guilt and shame resurfaced and clenched at her chest with a fierce grip.

Reaching over, she grabbed her phone and started to get out when the text message she'd received earlier grabbed her attention. It was from an unknown number.

Not so perfect anymore, are you, Nora?

Chapter Thirteen

Nora raced up to her room through the back entrance. The tiny set of stairs had been made for future renovations of a studio in the attic. A studio that never came. Her dad had hoped to one day get back to his writing and wanted a space where he could come and go without distraction. The attic never was converted and was still the bare bones it was when the place was built, minus a few boxes to the side. A door set in a little alcove before the stairs started the last leg to the attic. Nora opened it and peered down the hallway. The coast was clear. Shutting the door with a quiet click, she rushed down to her room. Her parents didn't know how lucky they were. With an escape route like that, it would be easy for the girls to sneak out and back in without ever being detected. Lucky for her parents, they never had anywhere to go.

With sweat building on her forehead, Nora tossed her phone onto the bed and ran her hands through her hair. What was she going to do? How did they get her number? Better yet, who? None of this was making sense. What had she ever done to earn this attention? To be blamed for *murder*? Sitting down at her desk, she opened herself up.

What have I done? she screamed inside her head as she searched through her memories. Years of laughter as a child. Her parents drifting apart. Taking care of Beth. Keeping her head high. Aiming for her best and being ruthless on the debate platform. She opened herself further, not wanting to miss or believe she was some perfect thing she wasn't. But no matter how hard she searched, how hard she pushed, she couldn't find anything besides the few weeks she was hateful to Beth before her incident. There was no way Beth was behind all of this, was there?

The bile in her stomach rolled and started to rise. She ran for her bathroom and almost didn't make it before throwing up what little she'd eaten that day. Sitting back on the coral tile, she ran a hand over her forehead to wipe away the sweat. It couldn't be Beth. Beth wouldn't do that to her. *Manic episodes.* The reminder from Dr. Woods seeped into her mind and she felt like she was going to be sick again.

First Liv and Charlie, then Reed, and now *Beth*! Why was she blaming everyone around her? It could be some random person at school or a neighbor down the street or a bus boy she looked at funny. *Paranoia is one of the first major symptoms.*

"No," she whispered. Then over and over again she repeated the mantra, almost to the point she was screaming. She was not losing her mind. Beth had nothing to do with this. She was not losing her mind. She wasn't! She was fine!

Strong hands gripped her shoulders and it was then that she heard her mother's frantic panic. "Nora, sweetie, what's the matter?"

A sob ripped from Nora's throat and she hunched in on herself. This couldn't be happening. It couldn't. She gripped the sides of her head with both hands while her mom pulled her forward into her arms.

"Please talk to me, baby. What's wrong?" The terror in her mom's voice shook Nora. The memories of her mom worried and pouring herself another glass of wine as she looked at Beth, feeling helpless and the burden of that motherly instinct to help her child though she didn't know how.

Nora sat up and wiped the tears from her face. She didn't want to be that burden. If she was going to lose her mind, or was in the process of doing so, she might as well get a jump start. "I'm scared," she admitted. "And I hate myself for what I'm scared of."

Her mom rubbed her hands up and down her back. "Honey, you can tell me anything."

She doubted that. She didn't think her mom would be 'okay' if she was to tell her she was being setup for murder or that it mimicked a murder she had plotted for funzies with her friends. Still, she knew this was one thing she could tell her mom. She sniffled, then said, "I don't want to be crazy."

Her mom smiled and cupped her chin to better look her in the eyes. "Honey, we're all a little crazy."

A light air floated through Nora and she smiled. The coral tile was cool under her legs. "Even on our best days." It had been something her grandmother had said to her mother when they went to visit her last year. Nora's mom had yelled at her grandma, proclaiming she was crazy.

Holding her head high, her grandma said, "Even on my best days." The reminder brought a smile to both of them.

Settling in her mother's arms, Nora confided in her about her fears she had of becoming like Beth. It wasn't easy. Saying you didn't want to end up like your sister seemed like one of the harshest things a sibling could say. But her mom silenced all of that.

"There is nothing wrong with fearing something you hate. You see the struggle your sister endures and I'm sure you hate it for her."

"I do," Nora answered. She would do anything for Beth not to have to deal with it.

"With that hate comes a great sadness that leads to fear, especially since it's your sister. It's no different than an adult fearing a heart attack after hearing of someone close to them experiencing one. They hate that it happened to the other person, but they don't want it to happen to them. It natural, honey, and it doesn't mean you love her any less." She brushed Nora's hair back behind her ear. The warmth of her mom's love seeped into her. "You feel better?"

She did, other than the nagging ache in her core. She couldn't focus on feeling sorry for herself anymore. If she was going crazy, then so be it. She'd get the autograph prescription later. Right now, she had to focus on who was playing behind the scenes of her life. "Mom, do you think Beth is capable of doing something horrible, something you know she wouldn't do in her right mind?"

Her mom adjusted herself on the hard tile. Nora's butt was starting to go numb from sitting there. "I want to think not, but we've seen her episodes where she becomes almost suicidal. Honey, why do you think I've locked myself in this house for the past three years?"

A flush of guilt stormed through Nora. "To keep an eye on Beth," she whispered. The admission burned in her throat. All that time Nora thought it was because of her father. All those glasses of wine and tears shed as she looked out the sitting room window wrapped in a blanket. She'd thought her mother was pining over the loss and warmth of her husband's love. She'd really been trying to deal with the worry she held for her daughter.

Her mom tightened her arms around Nora. "It's also why your dad took on so many clients and stayed at the office. He didn't know how to face it." She kissed the top of Nora's head before standing to her feet and stretched.

"And you were okay with that?" Nora asked, looking up at her mom. She couldn't imagine being okay with it, not when you needed the support the most.

"I wasn't okay with it, not at all, but I didn't know how to confront him about it. I was doing what I had to do, living on the edge of my fears while watching you and Beth like prisoners, wanting to control what I couldn't. He was doing the same, dealing with his fears the only way he felt comfortable. It just… wasn't how I thought it should be done." She smiled down at Nora. "Then you come along and bite my head off." Nora opened her mouth to apologize but her mom bent down and placed a single finger over her lips. "And I will be forever grateful for that. It woke up a part of me that had been suppressed for a long time. I'd let the fear of what *might* happen rob me of the time I got *now* with you girls and your father. He had done the same." She pulled Nora into a tight hug. "I'm going to do my everything to remember that from now on. So is your father. I hadn't realized how… stale our lives had really gotten until you reminded me. The going to the lodge and then pushing me to wake up." She kissed the top of Nora's head. "I only wish I'd snapped out of it years ago."

Nora rushed to her feet and hugged her mom with everything she had inside of her. She wished she could tell her what caused all this, but she couldn't. Her mom may understand some things, but that she wouldn't. The first thing she would want to do after finding out her daughter was some crazed girl dreaming up fake murders to solve for practice and fun would be to go to the police. The police were a dead end for Nora and her friends. Her mom may not see it that way. It was a risk Nora wasn't willing to take, not yet.

"Oh god," her mom said as they stepped out of the bathroom and back into Nora's poorly lit room. She hadn't had time to flip on the lamps before losing her breakfast. "I left that poor boy downstairs."

"Boy?" Nora heart hitched. *He wouldn't have, would he?* She thought about Reed chasing her out of the library. *Oh God, he so would.*

"Reed?" her mom said, the questions heavy in her eyes. "I left him downstairs to come tell you he was here. And then… well…" She trailed off, not really caring to relive the moment of finding her daughter hysterical on the floor, smelling of vomit.

Nora leaned against the side of her chair for support. "Did he say what he wanted?"

Her mom shook her head. "All he said was that he needed to speak to you." The side of her mom's lips tilted up in an evil grin. "He's cute."

"Mom!" Nora protested. "It is not like that, at all." Her face betrayed her as heat rose up to her cheeks, setting them on fire. Her mom's smile widened. "Okay, he's a little cute, but we're not like dating or whatever."

Concern creased her brow. "Do you know what he wants?"

Nora had a pretty good idea. "Probably something to do with homework." She thought back to their encounter at the library and the way she'd run out on him. There was no coming back from that. What would she even say to him? "Can you just tell him I'm not feeling well and that I'll see him on Monday?"

Indecision weighed on her mother's face. She crossed her arms as she thought it over. When she looked at Nora with regret, Nora knew she'd lost. "I'm sorry, but I can't. They just issued a blizzard warning until two in the morning. I can't send him out in this. Where does he even live?"

Nora tensed. What would her mom think of him once she realized he was from the other side of town? There was no need in lying and she knew it. Her mom was a nosy person by nature and could casually bring it up while he was here. Reed was not ashamed of where he was from, as he shouldn't be. "West Heights."

The reaction she got wasn't one she expected. "That's too far. I'm sorry, but your friend is going to have to stay here." All this time, the way her mother acted, Nora thought it was her mom thinking she was some hoity toity and was better than everyone, when in reality she was drowning in fear. It had closed her off from the world, from reality. Before things started to go south, her mom hadn't acted high and mighty; neither had her father. Nora had just assumed with all the extra work her dad was getting and all the extra money that they were turning into snobs. She hadn't realized their parental love was taking a beating. Yes, her father pushed her to be academically achieved, but that was for her benefit, no one else's.

You know what they say, she chastised herself. *Assume and you shall be an ass.*

Sympathy shone on her mom's face. "But I can tell him you're sick. He can relax in the den."

Nora knew that wasn't what needed to happen. She needed to face the music and get this over with. Plus, if they were going to be snowed in under the same roof, they might as well get some brainstorming done while they were at it. That's if he didn't try walking home in the worst storm of the year after she told him the truth. "Can you send him on up?"

Her mom was skeptical. "Are you sure?"

"I'm sure," she said, already shaking from the thought of him being in her room. Before her mom stepped out of the room Nora asked, "Can I keep the door closed? There are some things I need to explain that I don't want Beth hearing." When her mom still held that questioning look, she rushed on. "I kind of freaked out on him and owe an explanation."

She was sure her mom was still going to say no, but then understanding and what she perceived as trust crossed over her face. "Okay, but I'll be checking in on you guys. So, there's that."

Nora laughed and thanked her mom before brushing her teeth and setting out to pickup her room. It wasn't like she had much to clean, but the bra and discarded panties had to go. That was a line of embarrassment she would rather avoid.

She sat down on the bed and waited. Ten seconds later she moved to the window seat to gaze at the snow. It didn't feel right either. She felt like a princess out of a movie gazing out the window and waiting for the boy to arrive. It was too Disney. Casual. She needed casual. She stood to move to her big chair when a knock came at the door. She stumbled but managed to grab a book from her pile next to the bed on her way down in the chair. She landed with her leg draped over the side and scrambled to open the book as Reed stepped inside.

"Hey," he said, taking in her room. His eyes lingered on the open space to the right of the room. "Nice, though it wasn't what I was expecting."

She managed to untangle herself from the awkward position in her chair and sat up straighter. "And what was that?" she challenged.

Reed shoved his hands into his back pockets and leaned against the door. His eyes bore into Nora and she thought she was going to be sick again. "Ruffles, maybe one of those curtain things around the bed."

She took a deep breath. She needed to relax. This was no different than if they were sitting on a bench outside school. Except that it was. "A canopy." Nora tucked the book away under her chair and then wrapped her arms around her legs. "And I'm not five, nor do I want to be a princess."

He pushed off the door and took a few steps toward her. "Yeah, I didn't peg you for that type." He picked up one of the books discarded on the floor. Books were scattered all over her room. "I also didn't peg you for a true crime fan."

Her eyes narrowed as he opened the book and started flipping through it. "What did you peg me for, romance and day dreams?" Not that she didn't have day dreams, but they weren't the kind you bragged about.

He considered her question. "Honestly, I thought of you as a historical fiction and nonfiction girl."

A gust of wind pushed at the window as snow pelted the glass. The wind was whipping the snow around so harshly she couldn't see down into her yard. "You'd be wrong," she said and picked up another book off the windowsill. "I like mystery and psychology. I'm only interested in history when it comes to keeping an A in class so I can get out of this town."

"God, don't tell me you want to go to the city too." The city reference was a common one and one everyone understood. To people other than those who lived in New York the state, when someone said New York in conversation they automatically thought of the Big Apple. They didn't consider the rest of the three-hundred-mile-wide state. It was also common to hear people want to move to the city around there. It seemed to be the big achievement for everyone. Everyone but Nora... and maybe Reed.

"Think warmer and farther west." The brochure of the warm campus setting, with a plush green yard stared up at her. She had received it in the mail the other day after requesting an application and scholarship information. She had yet to show it to anyone. "They have some of the best rankings for their criminology program." Her stomach twisted as she handed him the brochure. What would he think of her now?

"Criminology, huh?" He looked the brochure over and then looked up at her as if seeing her for the first time. She leaned against her bookshelf to tether herself to the now. She felt like she was being weighed and measured, and while it made her nervous, she liked it. Showing who she truly was made her feel alive and real. "Ya know, that makes more sense."

The admission takes her by surprise. "It does?" Doubt crept in her. Did he know about the Murder Mystery Club?

Was that why it made sense? Nora eased away from him. "How?"

He set the brochure back on her desk, then picked up her favorite psychology book. It was full of quotes and small perspectives, much like a poetry book, and she'd read every line in there at least five times. It was her bible. "Yeah. The debate team, your sudden interest in Kyle, seeing you today in the true crime section. It's all starting to add up."

He had no idea. The reminder of today made her blush. This was going to be the beginning of the spiral. "Yeah, about that... I'm sorry for the way I bolted today. I don't want you to think I'm crazy."

"Too late," he said with a smile. "Seriously though, you don't owe me an explanation. I came here to make sure you were okay, nothing more, nothing less. What I didn't expect was to get trapped due to the weather." He peered out the window and up to the sky. "They say it's not supposed to let up for a while."

"Mom said it could be the middle of the night." She came to stand next to him at the window. "Did you call your grandma?"

Pulling his phone out of his pocket, he scrolled through his call history. "I tried, but I couldn't get through. Land lines must be down and she never has her cell phone turned on while she's home."

"Hopefully she turns it on soon, just to call you if nothing else." A tree branch snapped from the single tree outside of her window and slammed into the side of the house. Nora jerked. "You know, life doesn't always go as we expect and sometimes that drives us to lose our mind. I lost my mind today and I'm sorry." She nudged him with her shoulder. "And thanks for coming to check on me, even though it cost you getting trapped to do so."

He looked at her out of the corner of his eye. "I can think of worse places to be trapped."

She acknowledged that with a smile but didn't lose her train of thought. She needed to get this out and really talk about it. Keeping her focus on the twisted branches outside, she continued, "The murders have gotten to me. It's made me start to question everything."

"That's normal," he said and crossed his arms over his middle. "It's close to home and you start to wonder things and question everything. I have been." He turned to the side to face her, but she remained facing the window. She was afraid if she looked at him, she would lose her nerve. "Tell me, what's one of the things you've been asking yourself relentlessly."

The white outside began to fade into a blur as she squeezed her arms tighter around herself. Her eyes were focused on the outside world while her mind was focused on the admission she was about to whisper. "Why someone would want to frame me for murder?"

Her bedroom door banged open and Beth came barging inside. "Excuse me?"

Chapter Fourteen

After calming Beth down and shutting the door so their mother couldn't hear, she sat Reed and Beth down. Beth curled up in the chair like a cat. It was her shield. She knew whatever Nora was about to tell them was big and she needed all the defenses she could get. Nora had witnessed her sister in the same position several times over the past few years while sitting in her therapist's office. It worried Nora and made her question whether she should be saying anything or not. Could Beth handle it?

Reed sat perched on the windowsill, aware and ready. Between Reed and Beth, she knew he was going to be the one she looked to the most. It wasn't that she needed his approval. It was that he was already aware something was happening and was ready to fill in the holes. He could help her. Beth was fixing to take a shock to the system.

"About six months ago, I met with these two girls." So started the story. Nora told Reed and Beth about Liv and Charlie, how she had met them in the M&M chat online. They'd both been silent about the club, seeming more surprised by the concept of it than the interest of Nora being involved. It wasn't until she told them Liv and Charlie had decided to meet in person that Beth came alive.

"Are you insane?" she asked, sitting up in her chair. She knocked over a stack of books by Nora's bed and they slid across the floor. Beth started picking them up. "Obviously, you are. Why do you always have a stack of books by your bed?"

"How else do you plan for me to fall asleep?"

"I don't know." Beth slammed a book on top of the stack. "Quit obsessing over murder."

Nora collapsed on the bed. Here it came. The real storm. The storm of her anger and misunderstanding. "I wasn't obsessing over it." Beth gave Nora the look; the one that told her Beth didn't believe her. "It's what I'm passionate about, Beth."

"About death? Do you know how insane that sounds?" It did sound insane and Nora couldn't deny it.

"It's not the death part. God, I'm not a monster. It's the tick, the why and how behind it. The mystery." She was sure it didn't sound any better, but it was the truth behind it. What made a person operate behind the mask?

Beth picked up another one of her criminal psychology books. "That is not normal," Beth screamed. "No wonder someone is trying to frame you for murder. You're an easy target."

"At least I'm passionate about something!" Nora snapped. When Beth turned around, her face drawn, Nora instantly regretted it. Why had she said that? She hadn't snapped at Beth since the incident before the birthday party. "Beth, I'm☐"

"No," she said, holding up her hand. "You're right. I'm only passionate about myself, right?" She ran her finger along the book spines in the shelf above her desk. *How the Mind Works. Inside the Criminal Mind. Without Conscience.*

Evil. Forensic Psychology. An Unquiet Mind. Manic. Madness: A Bipolar Life. The titles started to shift from criminal psychology to bipolar disorders. Beth halted on the *Manic* title but didn't pull it out. "I think I'm starting to see."

Nora glanced at Reed who was hunched forward, his elbows resting on his knees, and his head bowed. It was the most he could do to give them privacy without awkwardly leaving the room. Nora didn't want to have this conversation in front of him. She didn't want to tell her sister how she had discovered that some of the most notorious serial killers in the world had been diagnosed with bipolar depression. She didn't want to tell her sister that she was fascinated by it because she wanted to and hoped to figure the mind out one day to prevent the next murder from happening. She didn't want to tell Beth she was afraid of what might happen to her one day if they didn't keep her symptoms in check in front of Reed. *Or what might have already happened,* she thought to herself. She shoved that thought aside. She would find time to talk to Beth later, when it was just the two of them.

"M&M, which was closely scripted like D&D, had been great. It helped me escape and learn, and kept my mind occupied, until that Thursday." Nora shuttered at the memory of Liv texting her to tell her about Kyle. She did know that she would ever shake the memory of that moment. The moment that started her on this path.

"The night Kyle died," Reed muttered. He got up from his seat near the window and leaned against the bookshelf. It seemed no one could sit still. "How did that get you involved?" he asked, having already known something was up.

"It mimicked the case I had created earlier that day at our meeting." She went on to explain how they took turns creating murder scenes, had to create clues, a witness list, a suspect list, all of it.

"And you picked Kyle as your victim that day?" Reed asked.

The feel of the pen striking through all the descriptions she had written out for Gary, her original victim, and replacing them with Kyle's information. She had to go through and strike out quite a few evidence markers, hair here or there, on a lot of her note cards. She couldn't help but wonder what would have happened if she'd never used Kyle to begin with. Would he still be alive? Would Gary be dead instead? Gary had been her original victim.

Reed ran his fingers through his brown hair. He had a slight wave to his locks that caused some of the hair to stick up when ruffled. "Everything about your case you'd built was used to stage Kyle's death."

"I don't think everything," she said, thinking back to the witnesses she'd wrote out. "I never heard anything about him getting into a fight or seeing a friend before being murdered. Did you?"

He scratched at his face, where a prickle of facial hair was starting to show. Nora spaced out imagining what he would look like with a beard. She couldn't deny he would look damn sexy. Realizing she was spacing, she focused back in on what he was saying. "…maybe that will tell us, right?"

Why did he have to end it with a question? "Sure."

Beth rolled her eyes and puffed out a harsh breath when Nora didn't go on to provide more information. "Well, who was the killer?"

"Oh, the old lady who was at the gas station. Kyle had crossed paths with her one too many times and that night he had stolen her spot in line for gas. Her reasoning was she was 'tired of people like him in the world. Inconsiderate brats.' She was a total nut job." She fought not to glance at Beth. She'd read several past cases where people had snapped before murdering someone. On most occasions, it was irrational thoughts that lead them to overreacting.

"And totally fake," Beth chimed in. "We don't know if Kyle had a crazy old lady tailing him."

Reed deflated. "No, I guess not."

She thought about the message she'd received earlier. It had been personal. "What do you think about the text message?" Nora asked.

"What text message?" Reed and Beth asked at the same time. Nora jerked up, sure she had told them. Maybe she had day-dreamed that too. She needed to pull herself together.

"Sorry," she said as she went to get her phone off the middle of the bed. "I thought I told you already." She pulled up the messages. "It could be nothing," she said, handing the phone over.

Reed read over it first. "This is not nothing, Nora. When did you get this?"

"After I left the library." The admission burned in the back of her throat. Or was that another wave of vile ready to come up? Looking at Beth, she wasn't so sure. Reed seemed to get it and didn't make mention of the why about it. Nora turned her attention on Beth, fearing what she may think it meant.

Beth, however, didn't get the connection. Thank God. She never wanted her sister to find out the fear she held inside of her. She wanted Beth to feel safe and loved around her. It was Nora's own problem to hash out and understand. No matter what happened, she was never going to abandon her sister because of fear. She also marked her off as a suspect. There was no way Beth could have killed Kyle. Looking at her small frame and knowing her I-like-to-keep-to-myself attitude, she was sure Beth hadn't done it. If the day came and she was proven wrong, well, then she'd eat crow.

"I'll be back," Beth said, heading for the door with Nora's phone clutched tight in her hand.

"Where are you going?" Nora asked, needing a little explanation as to where her phone was going. It wasn't like she had much of a life in there, but she still wanted to be in the know.

Beth opened the door but didn't look back over her shoulder at Nora. "Guess you weren't the only one with a secret passion. I can hack this baby and see if I can get a trail on the number that sent it to you. It may take me a few hours."

"Okay," Nora said, hoping her sister could figure it out but also wishing they had confided in each other sooner. If there was one thing this had taught Nora, it was that she needed to learn to be more open with the people she loved.

Once Beth stepped out of the room and shut the door, the quiet settled in on Nora and Reed. "You know," he said, going over to the desk and grabbing a pen and piece of paper. "It might help if we play a little M&M of our own, see if we can narrow down a suspect list."

Nora agreed. After she was done telling him all the names the librarians had given her, she told him about Charlie's suspicion. "What about Liv? Did she say anything?"

Nora shook her head. "She's caught up in a little drama with Charlie right now. Charlie thinks Liv may have something to do with it now."

"What?" Reed asked, surprised. "I'm surprised to hear that. Those two are really close."

"Yeah, I know." Nora went to grab for her phone and then realized it wasn't there. "Dang it. Usually I don't need it and the one time I want to check in with Liv it's gone."

Reed smiled over at her. "That's how it usually works."

They bantered back and forth about the pros and cons of each name they had on their suspect list. Nora had purposefully left Beth's name off the list. She wasn't going to involve her sister in a friendly banter of debate. Nora was sure Beth had nothing to do with this.

As it turned out, Reed knew a lot about the people on the list from the library. Mr. Rivets was a widower who had retired a year before his wife passed away from cancer. He lived alone with plenty of money but went to the library for human interaction. Reed's grandpa often went over to play cards with Mr. Rivets, along with a few other men from the neighborhood. Ms. Humphrey was a simple old lady who liked her jig saw puzzles as complicated as she liked her soap operas. She walked with a cane on most days due to her hip surgery a few years prior, but she tried to manage without it, especially when in public. Neither one of them sounded or fit the profile of someone who had brutally beat and sliced on Kyle before discarding him in the lake.

Nora asked about Mrs. Segmeyer, though Charlie had already crossed her off their list. Reed had done the same. Apparently, Mrs. Segmeyer spent her time away from her kids working at the homeless shelter. If she wanted to murder anyone, it would be someone no one would miss.

"What about... I don't know... street gangs he hung around with?"

Reed's face said it all. *Was she being for real right now?* "You mean those convenience store, Twizzler-stealing thieves?"

"Hey, Twizzler's can be the first stepping stone into a life of crime."

Amusement shone in Reed's eyes. "Stepping stone, not a leap across the Grand Canyon. Someone doesn't go from stealing a Twizzler to killing someone like that. Besides, have you ever met any of these so-called gang members?" Nora shook her head. How would she have met them? "Well, I have, and let me tell you, they're wannabes. One of the girls in the gang got a Principal Scholar Award two weeks ago."

Oh! Nora had been hoping to find out otherwise. Frustration ran through Nora and she sprawled out on the bed. A frustrated growl ripped through her chest. "Who are you and what do you want?" She stared up at her ceiling, hoping the answer would click. That's how it normally happened, right? How am I going to do this? Two hours later, click! Here are your answers. It'd been well over two hours and was spilling into weeks. Where was her click?

Reed sat down on the bed next to her. "Hey, we're going to figure this out. In the meantime, trust no one and suspect everybody."

Nora propped herself up on her elbow. If he only knew how high her paranoia was right now. "What about you?" she asked with a challenge. "Where were you when Kyle died?"

Reed leaned back, closer to her. "I was out stealing Twizzlers," he whispered.

Laughter bubbled out of her, hard and fast. Her stomach soon hurt, but she couldn't stop. "I haven't laughed like that in a long time," she gasped once she was able to catch her breath.

"You should," he said. "I like your laugh."

Nora's insides flamed. Of all the things she should be focusing on, his eyes shouldn't be one of them. She had an unknown number sending her cryptic messages. Said same person could be the killer behind two teen deaths. Liv and Charlie weren't talking to each other. And considering what happened in her bathroom two hours ago, she was sure she wasn't in a stable frame of mind. Yet, here she was, staring at his mouth and wondering what it would be like to be kissed.

He rested back on his elbow, bringing them face to face. He licked his lips, his gaze intense. Nora had to shake herself to focus. "I meant what I said, Nora. We're going to figure this out and I'm here for you until we do."

All she could manage to do was nod her appreciation. If she opened her mouth to express her thanks, she wasn't sure what stuttering mess would come out. It was nice having someone in her corner. That was a relief that eased her mind. The next step was finding out who murdered Kyle and Ryan, and why.

They laid side by side on the bed talking. It amazed Nora how lost in conversation she could get with Reed and not even realize it. It was easy. She didn't find herself scrambling through a questionnaire trying to figure out the next stance in the conversation. She just talked. He talked. The conversation flowed.

As it turned out, Reed wanted to go into law enforcement. He didn't care to be in the military like his parents. Yes, it was an honorable lifestyle, but not one he saw for himself. He mentioned his frustration with his parents, and Nora knew that was the root for him. It was what kept him from wanting that lifestyle for himself. The resentment.

"Have you ever thought of going into a higher branch of law enforcement?" Nora asked.

"What, you mean like FBI or something?"

She nodded.

"Not really. I don't know that I want to leave my grandparents. Someone needs to be here for them. Small town cop may be all I have in me." It was honorable and Nora found herself melting even further into all things that were Reed Benson.

"I'm sorry," she whispered, and felt the hot sting of tears building. She'd felt pain and regret before when she'd hurt Beth, but this was different. She took a deep breath, trying to understand what she was feeling. She had judged him for so long, hadn't given him the time of day to see who he was. Instead, she had judged from afar and kept her distance. The pain of that truth, of the terrible person she could be, and how she fit with the others at Pinewood ripped at her chest.

Reed reached over and wiped the tear from her cheek before it could make it to her comforter. "For what?" he asked, a little confused by her sudden breakdown.

She hated the feeling churning in her gut. "For getting it wrong." She thought of Beth and the fear she held inside of losing herself to the same things Beth endured. "I've misunderstood so much in my life. Everyone thinks I'm smart, but I'm not."

Reed started to reach out and pull her to him but stopped. "Is it okay if I... hold you?"

The question took her off guard. She hadn't realized how much she was drowning until that moment. She needed the raft and wanted to be pulled into comfort more than anything.

She nodded and Reed wrapped his arms around her, pulling her gently against him. "I'm going to tell you right now, no one is perfect. No matter how hard they try, one day their kingdom is going to crumble under the fake mortar they've built themselves on. Being real," he said, brushing back her hair and looking into her eyes, "and feeling the hurt, the pain, and the regret, it's what makes us human. It's what teaches us life. The lesson is deciding what you learn."

Nora sniffled, not knowing what to say under that wisdom... or his stare. "What makes you so wise?"

"I'm a Twizzler thief, remember? My grandmother chewed my ass a lot."

Nora's mom peeked her head inside and seemed unsettled by the sight of seeing Reed holding her daughter. She prompted him to the couch in the den. Nora noted it was the furthest room from her room. In between was probably her mother, sipping a glass of wine and reading a book.

The thought crossed her mind that the stairs in the back led to the back door. Around back and across the patio was another door that led to the den. She could sneak down there and talk the night away. She glanced out the window at the howling wind and snow. Reed could wait until tomorrow. Nora snuggled down into her blankets, a smile of contentment on her face.

Chapter Fifteen

The room was bright in the early morning hours. Nora pulled the comforter up to her chin, the chill of the night air lingering in her room. She'd forgotten to close her curtains before falling asleep to the hypnotic waves of the snow blowing past the glass. Slowly, like a turtle crawling through the desert, the memories of last night started creeping into her thoughts. She pushed up, remembering Reed was in the den. She couldn't leave him to the devise of her parents.

After brushing her teeth and changing clothes, Nora rushed downstairs. The smell of coffee wafted up over the banister. Was she already too late? There was no telling what kind of questions her parents would ask him. She was surprised when she burst through the kitchen to find no one there. *Who had started the coffee?* The smell of the coffee was tempting and Nora poured herself a cup. She usually refrained from drinking coffee on Sundays. She liked to be as chilled as possible.

"Hey," Reed said, coming into the kitchen. His voice was thick with sleep and there was a crinkle from the couch imprinted on his face. "Mind if I get a cup?"

"Sure." She reached up into the cabinet to grab him a mug. "Did you sleep well?"

"Honestly, no." He took the mug from her and poured the delicious brown liquid inside. When she offered him the creamer, he waved her off. "Straight up. It fills the veins faster." Nora showed him the pastry bin full of muffins, bagels, and doughnuts.

"Dang. This is nice. I should invest in a pastry bin."

Nora took a bite of her glazed doughnut. "If there's one thing I can't live without in this house, it's the pastry bin. I'd lose my mind." Nora washed her dish and rinsed out her mug. "So, why couldn't you sleep."

Reed took a tentative sip of his coffee. "I was thinking about our list. I know you don't want to hear this, but I think you need to keep an eye on Gary."

"Gary?" That had not been what she was expecting. Gary was not even on her radar anymore. He was good as gold. "Reed, I'll tell you the same thing I told Charlie and Liv; there's no reason he would want to set me up for murder. He is better than me in every way."

"Not in every way," Reed muttered so low Nora had almost missed it. "You ever think he was secretly crushing on you or something?"

She doubled over laughing. He was the second person to suggest the ridiculous notion. Charlie and Reed didn't know Gary like she did. "Trust me, he does not like me like that."

"How do you know?" Reed reached around her to put his cup in the sink. "You seem to underestimate yourself in a lot of areas."

A blush fluttered through Nora and she had to fight to keep from stepping away from him. "Trust me, I'm not this time." She looked up at him, meeting his hazel eyes with her blue. *Don't back down. Stay strong.*

He leaned in an inch closer. "I think you are."

Nora wasn't sure what to say or how to react. She wasn't sure she could. Her throat felt tight and her body pulsed to move closer to him. Thankfully, she didn't have to see what embarrassing response she would have. Beth came sauntering into the room.

"Good morning, beautiful people." Nora and Reed broke apart, him going in the opposite direction as Beth. She laughed. "Don't stop on my behalf. Please, feel free to carry on."

Nora glared at Beth. "And how did you sleep, sister dear?"

"Wonderful, sister mine," she said in a sing-song voice. Nora wanted to strangle her.

Reed cleared his throat. "I'm going to get going. The plows have been out all morning. I'm sure the roads are drivable. My grandma's probably worried sick."

"Couldn't get a hold of her?" Nora asked.

Reed shrugged on his coat. "I tried, but still no answer." He grabbed another muffin from the pastry box. "One for the road," he said, holding it up as if it was some prized possession. The muffins were divine.

When Nora continued to stand there as Reed walked away, Beth shoved her sister hard in the shoulder. "Go see him out, you dunderhead."

Oh, right. Nora rushed to catch up with him. "I'll keep the advice about Gary in mind, but I really don't think he's anything to worry about."

"I'm not so sure," he said while sweeping a scarf around his head. "Tell your mom I appreciate her letting me stay."

"I will," she said, not knowing what else to say. Where did she go from here? Why was it that she could construct whole murder scenes and defend or tear apart the oddest of topics behind a podium, yet she couldn't muster up how to have a conversation with a boy. "Stay safe out there." She wanted to melt into a puddle of pathetic slush once the words left her mouth. What was she eighty?

He opened the door and she figured the moment was over. They'd go back to their few texts here and there and life would be simple again. Before he stepped out the door, though, he paused and looked back at her. Before she could react, he leaned in and kissed her on the forehead. She was immobile against his body and breathed in the strong scents that were him. It reminded her of fresh air and sunny days, with a side of dirt and sweat.

"Thanks for confiding in me. I promise it's going to be okay." She shivered as his breath ruffled her hair. He gave her a soft hug, which she was happy to return. It was so nice to realize she now had the support she so much craved. "I'll call you later, okay?"

"Okay," she said as he walked out into the snow. When she got back into the kitchen, Beth was grinning so wide Nora was certain she saw her molars. "Turn the high beams off, will ya?"

"Sorry, I can't help it. He's cute," Beth swooned.

"He is." Nora wasn't going to deny it. Reed was cute, always had been. The difference now was her eyes were open and she no longer had the blinders of good and bad over her eyes. "But we're just friends."

Beth rolled her eyes and took a bite of her bagel. The cream cheese to bread ratio was poorly distributed. "You are so senile," she said, her mouth full of white cream. She waved the bagel around between bites. "And it's because of that your judgment of Gary has become null and void."

"Whatever," Nora sighed. "Were you able to figure anything out on my phone?"

Beth looked annoyed. "No. Your phone is ancient. Have you ever thought about getting an upgrade?" An upgrade? She'd just got that phone six months ago. Seeing her face, Beth waved her bagel around. "Don't worry about it. I gave it an upgrade and put a tracking app on it. Unless they have blockers and I have to dig deeper, we should be fine." Beth finished off her bagel and got up to stand next to Nora. She placed her hand on her sister's shoulder. "Seriously, though, you need to watch your back. This invitation extends to Gary."

Nora's mood dropped, hard and fast. With all this talk about Gary, she was starting to believe maybe there was something to it, even if she didn't think there was.

Don't fool yourself. It's probably one of them. Enemy, close. Enough said.

Nora backed away from Beth and made an excuse of needing to study. Her thoughts were going in a direction she didn't like. She needed to escape and talk herself off the ledge. When she got to her room, she found a text from Reed waiting for her.

Reed: I had a great time last night.

Nora hit ignore and tossed her phone to the side. *Convenient that he came swooping in the way he did.*

She buried her head into the pillow and screamed.

Chapter Sixteen

Nora spent the better part of Monday morning avoiding Reed and watching Gary. Her mind was still reeling with thoughts of doubt while she heeded the warnings to watch her back. She had two morning classes with Gary and she spent every second watching him. The problem was, there was nothing to see. He poured himself over the texts assigned and kept conversations to a minimum. All the while, Nora cataloged every movement with intent. He didn't seem like someone out plotting her demise.

By the time lunch rolled around, she'd had enough. She stormed up to his locker and confronted him. He jerked back when he turned around to find her standing right behind him. "Nora. Is everything okay?"

No, everything was not okay. *Are you framing me for murder?* She wanted to scream at him. "Have you heard anything else about the police questioning us?"

He shouldered his backpack. "No, though I've been curious myself to know what progress they've made. Stacey told me she saw them in the office earlier, but I haven't heard of anyone getting pulled aside for questioning. Have you?"

She shook her head. "No, but it's driving me crazy. I've been thinking about it all weekend." A lot of things drove her crazy over the weekend, including Reed. She could feel his eyes on her down the hall, but she didn't dare look at him. She could only imagine what he was thinking while she talked with Gary.

Gary brushed past her. It was a blow off if she'd ever seen one. She almost laughed to herself. *There's no way this is a vying for your attention ploy.* He had her attention, yet he didn't seem to want it. "I'll let you all know if I hear anything." He started to leave, but then turned back to her. "Don't forget we have varsity in two weeks. Are you ready?"

The reminder startled her. She'd forgotten varsity was coming up. It was something she normally never took her sights off. "Yeah, I'll be ready."

He left her standing at his locker and made his way to the lunch room. She was sure he didn't have anything to do with the murders, this encounter being proof. He didn't even seem worried about not hearing from the police. *It could be a well thought out cover up.*

Reed was still standing at the other end of the hall, watching her, when Nora turned and went the other way. She needed some fresh air and time to think. Her mind kept telling her things she knew weren't true. Beth being at the center of it. Reed only being her friend to find out what she knows. Gary finding her insignificant and not worth his time. The thoughts were full of turmoil and made her feel sick inside. Was this what Beth dealt with every day as she faced her peers? Was her mind full of nothing but doubts and fears?

A flush of warmth spread out from Nora's stomach and she doubled over, sure she was going to throw up. Her heart hammered in her chest so fast she was sure it would explode. She was almost to her bench when another wave of warmth flashed through her, and this time, she did get sick. She leaned over in the bushes and let the acid and water that filled her stomach come tumbling out.

Her hair was suddenly swept off her neck and held back out of the danger zone. Reed's soft voice told her she was okay and that she needed to breathe between retches. She did as he said, and once she was sure she wasn't going to throw up again, she stood straight and let the world around her spin. Her stomach was weak, and her heart still pounded in her chest.

"I feel like I'm unraveling," she whispered while she let Reed guide her to the bench.

"It's okay." He started rubbing small circle of comfort across her back. "Take deep breaths. Focus on those breaths and tell yourself you're here in the moment. Ground yourself."

Nora did as he said, and after several deep breaths, her heart started to slow its pace. Her stomach was still twisted, but she no longer felt the strong urge to throw up. She leaned forward and rested her head in her hands. "What is happening to me?"

"It's the worry of the unknown." He let her hair fall around her face, shielding her. "Was this your first panic attack?"

Nora shook her head. There was the bathroom incident earlier. Plus, she'd seen Beth experience them on several different occasions. "Why is this happening to me?" she whined then hated herself for it.

"You worrying about the who behind the murders is probably what triggered it." He continued to rub her back. Snow from the storm Saturday night was still thick on the ground but was starting to melt. Nora had never been so thankful for the chill in the air as she was right then. "My grandma used to have them all the time when my mom would leave for another tour. She's better now."

"How?" Nora asked. She thought once someone opened the door to panic attacks there was no shutting it off.

"Medicine. Yoga. Liquor." Reed smiled down at her and held out a stick of gum. "That seems to be her favorite method."

Nora took the gum. "Great. All I need to do is become a raging alcoholic." The panic was starting to set in again. "I'm sorry," she said, realizing how terrible that sounded. "I just... I didn't realize this was what it was like. The panic." Had this been what Beth was experiencing for the past three years? "It's pretty intense."

"Talking with Gary is probably what triggered it," Reed commented. "Extreme levels of stress are usually what kick it off." She knew that. The birthday party had been Beth's stress trigger. "What did Gary have to say, anyway?"

He was going to be pleasantly disappointed when she told him the big no news. "Said he hadn't heard anything, but that Stacey had heard the cops were here again today." She took another deep breath, her skin still hot from the rush of adrenaline. "I hope that's more myth than fact."

Sitting back against the bench, she looked at Reed. Really looked at him. He seemed sincere – like he was willing to help her figure this out. The problem for her was the doubt lingering inside of her. It didn't make sense for him to want to help her. They'd never been friends before Kyle's death. Why now? Sure, she'd been nice to him after Kyle's death and they'd talked a few times, but was that grounds enough for risking life and limb like he seemed so willing to do?

She needed some real answers. "Reed, I need to know something, and I need a real answer. The last few days I've been struggling with the back and forth of doubt and hope. The only way to find out the truth, I guess, is to ask you." She took a steady breath and met his level stare. "Why are you suddenly interested in helping me?"

Reed sat back, but never took his eyes off her. It was as if he was daring her to look away first. She didn't. She needed to know what his intentions were and the only way to do that was to take a look into his soul. "I⬚"

"We need Ms. Fletcher to the office. Ms. Fletcher to the office." Dammit to hell. She looked toward the front of the building, knowing what was waiting for her inside. The police.

Reed forgot about what he was going to say and grabbed her hand. "No matter what they say to you, stay strong. Don't let them scare you. If they get too pushy, ask for your dad. They can't question you further if you ask for your parents." Nora nodded and felt a wave of heat start to build in her stomach. The panic was playing peek-a-boo.

She stood and started for the building, but Reed hadn't let go of her hand. He stood and pulled her back to him. When she turned to look at him, she saw heat inside of his eyes. Running his hands up her arms, he cupped her face. "And to answer your question, honestly, I first started questioning you because I knew you were hiding something. I didn't know what it was, but I knew it had something to do with Kyle's death. I thought..." He closed his eyes for the briefest of seconds. "I thought maybe you had killed him." When she gasped and started to step back, he caressed her cheeks with his thumbs and looked her deep in the eyes. "But then I talked to you and I knew there was no way a girl as great as you are, who wonders about life and all the clicks it takes to make it work, could kill someone. You're too passionate about life to bring death. Once I realized that, I could have walked away, but then... I heard your laugh and felt your pain and knew there was no place on this earth I would rather be than right by your side." He leaned his forehead against hers. "I couldn't walk away," he whispered.

Heat rose up in her cheeks and she let the tension she held in her body go. She let her emotions take the lead and run her body for her. This she didn't want control over. Her hands ran up his arms until their fingers collided in a tangle of promises. Her body softened against his and she relished in the heat of his body and the safety it offered. She was safe there, away from the panic and fear of who was watching her every move. Reed lowered his head and Nora stepped up to close the distance, their lips almost touching, when the intercom dinged again, bringing them out of their trance.

"Ms. Fletcher to the office. Ms. Fletcher to the office."

Nora pulled back and Reed made her promise to meet him at the water fountains after sixth period. On her way into the building, her phone buzzed in her back pocket. She pulled it out to find another text.

Unknown: Perfect lies often lead to perfect disasters.

What the hell is that supposed to mean? She filed the question away to mull over later. She then sent a quick text to Beth to let her know she'd received another text. Beth quickly responded and told her she was on it.

She was coming around the corner, almost to the office, when she ran into Kenzie McNosey. "Hey, watch it," she said and avoided touching Nora by side-stepping her and almost tripping over herself to do so. She glared at Nora. "I hear crazy rubs off like karma."

"Then I guess you don't have anything to worry about," Nora said, stepping closer so she was almost touching her. "Karma's already all over your ass and one day, you're going to have an ugly fall." She leaned in to whisper. "I only hope I'm there to see it."

Anger seeped off Kenzie in waves, but so did fear. She had been there at the party. Her younger cousin Lisa hadn't wanted to go alone so she'd begged Kenzie to go with her. Kenzie had stood off to the side and witnessed the whole thing. After, she'd helped spread the rumors and light the fire that Nora was next. She made Nora's life a living hell as often as she could. Just the other day she whispered 'murderer' as Nora passed her in the hallway. The only time Kenzie was a halfway decent human being was when her mother was around.

"You're such a freak, Fletcher," Kenzie said as she walked away, her steps a little faster.

"I'll be sure to pass the compliment along," she said to her retreating form. "Maybe tonight while your mother's over playing bridge." That stopped her in her tracks.

Kenzie turned, a flame of fury in the empty pastel colored hallway. "You wouldn't dare."

Nora wanted to call her bluff, but she was done with this childish behavior. "You're right, I wouldn't, because I'm not as crazy as you." She sauntered off on that note, letting the last line of defeat spur her on. It was a rarity to get the last line on Kenzie. Hopefully it gave her something long and hard to think about, though Nora highly doubted she would.

By the time Nora reached the office, her hands were clammy again. "Ah, Ms. Fletcher," Mrs. Vass said as she came through the door. "Mr. Higgins is waiting in his office for you."

Nora thanked the secretary as she walked past the desk and went to the principal's door. She gave it a light knock as she opened it with caution. When Mr. Higgins saw her standing there, he waved her on inside. His face was pinched with concern. Standing in the corner was Detective Garcia and Detective Taylor.

"Have a seat," Mr. Higgins instructed. As she did, Detective Taylor sat across from her like he had the time before.

"Hello, Nora," Taylor said. "How have you been since we last spoke?"

"Fine, I guess. I heard about the other murder in town, as well as the flyer put up blaming the debate team. Is that why you are here?" It was bold, but Nora wasn't holding back. She needed information and anything they let slip she was ready to devour, even at her own expense.

"It is," he answered. "Tell me, how did you feel when you saw the second flyer?"

What was this, therapy hour? "A little shocked. I mean, the kid was from West High. What does that have to do with our debate team?"

"That's what we are trying to find out," Taylor said. He was the good cop, the one who gently told you the first step in what the meeting was really about.

Nora wasn't surprised when Garcia stepped up, her arms crossed. "We do have a connection." Her voice was hard, her glare even harder. "You."

Mr. Higgins cleared his throat. "At this time, I would like to advise you, Nora, that you do not have to say anything further and have a right to ask for your parents or a lawyer."

Taylor glanced back over at Garcia. They had known the principal would have to warn Nora. Now, they had to work around it. With Garcia having already delivered the bad news, a delight she seemed to enjoy, she motioned for Taylor to go ahead.

"Nora, we have it under strong evidence that you are involved with two girls from West High." The way he said 'involved' made it sound like it was more than it was. "Is that correct?"

Panic started to set in Nora's veins again, but she remembered what Reed had said. Deep breaths, stand your ground, and ask for backup when you need it. She looked to Principal Higgins. "I'd like to call my father."

Taylor sat back in his chair, defeated, while Garcia glared at her from the corner. After calling her father, who made it clear she was not to say another word, she sat back and relaxed. She wasn't the defenseless, backed-in-a-corner girl they had hoped she was. What she did realize was she was going to have to find the real killer behind the scenes before she was strung up to hang.

Her father walked into the office and gathered her without a word to the police. Right behind him was their lawyer who addressed Taylor and Garcia for them. He explained that if they wanted to arrange a questioning, they would have to go through him to set up an appointment. Nora didn't get to hear Garcia's hot response. Her dad quickly escorted her out of the building. As they were leaving, she looked down the long hallway to the water fountain. Guess she wouldn't be meeting Reed after all.

Chapter Seventeen

"Thanks, Mom," Nora said before grabbing her coat and heading out the door. She'd been a prisoner for the last twenty-four hours, ever since her father came to pick her up at school, and she was ready to get out. It was funny, considering the hermit she used to be. She used to pray for days when she didn't have to go anywhere.

In a weird way, she had Gary to thank for her escape. He'd texted earlier that day with a reminder of a debate meeting. He needed everyone there, no exceptions. Mom and Dad had no choice but to let her go. What they didn't know was that the debate meeting wasn't for another hour.

Reed was waiting for her at The Corner Café downtown. When she took her seat, she was pleased to see he already ordered her a hot herbal tea. "Wasn't sure if that's what you wanted," he said, gesturing to the tea. "But I thought I would order you something caffeine free."

It was sad to say, but it was the most thoughtful gesture ever made toward her outside of family. After being diagnosed with anxiety, Beth had to cut caffeine out of her life. She snuck a little here or there, but for the most part she kept her life as decaf as possible. "Thanks," she said, taking a tentative sip. It was the perfect temperature to make her inside perk up. "I hope this isn't permanent," she said, holding up her tea. "It's not bad, but I like my coffee."

"There's decaf," he prompted.

"Okay, let me rephrase that. I like my real coffee."

Reed chuckled as he handed her the menu. The options at The Corner Café weren't grand, but the food was delicious. She always ordered the five-layer cheese sandwich with a side of tomato soup. It was delicious.

After ordering, to which Reed ordered the same thing, he leaned forward to give her his full attention. She squirmed under the intensity. She knew she wasn't that interesting. "So, what happened after you left the office yesterday?"

Nora took another sip of her tea. "I experienced a real parental hostage situation. I never thought the day would come." After, of course, her father had set her down in the living room and instructed her to tell him everything. "I told my parents about Liv and Charlie."

"M&M?" Unlike Beth, who often dropped a joke about the club, Reed never did. On some level, he seemed to get it.

Nora sighed. "I couldn't. It sounds so insane when I try to talk about it."

Reed chuckled. "It is insane." And here she was just thinking he understood. When he saw her face fall, he rushed on to explain. "Everything sounds insane to the person who is passionate about it. They are bursting with ideas and wanting to convey every inch of their passion to the person willing to listen that when they are done, they feel insane."

To know of such passion and insanity, one had to have experienced it. "Okay, tell me what secret insanity you're holding back."

Red heat spread out across Reed's face. The scruff Nora was growing accustomed to now gone, his skin smooth. "I'm a little bit of an artsy fartsy, as my grandpa jokes. He's supportive and buys me the equipment I need, so don't think he's not cool with it. I think he just likes saying fartsy."

Nora chuckled. "It's quite the word." Reed told her a little more about his photography and paintings. He liked capturing the still, quiet moments of nature and then later repainting the scene. "I've started selling the photographs and paintings as sets online to help kickoff that college career," he joked. He had no high plans for college, not unless Nora could convince him otherwise. "It's not much, but it's a start."

Nora's phone buzzed in her pocket. It was the fifteen-minute warning she'd given herself before having to leave Reed. She knew she'd get lost in conversation with him and before either one of them knew it, it was ten o'clock and the bar was closing. The thought of missing the meeting crossed her mind, but Gary would lose his mind. She wouldn't put it past him if he called her parents to find out where she was. Then she'd be in a load of trouble.

"Everything okay?" Reed asked.

"I have a debate meeting in a few minutes," she groaned.

"Do you need me to come with you?" It was a sweet gesture and she knew why he was making it. He still didn't trust Gary.

"Nah, it's boring stuff you want to miss, I promise." Varsity prep talk was no picnic. If Nora wasn't part of the varsity team, she wouldn't even be going.

"Was Beth able to find out anything on your phone?" He signaled for the waitress to come over and refill his water. Whether he ever planned to join the military or not, he had some healthy habits ingrained in him. Nora noticed the lines and contours of his arms under his dark green, long sleeved thermal shirt.

She opened her phone and pulled up the message she'd received yesterday. She hadn't been able to tell him about it or show him since being taken hostage by her father. "This was sent to me yesterday on my way to the office."

"What do you think it means?" he asked.

Nora had thought about it all night. *Perfect lies lead to perfect disasters.* She couldn't figure it out. "I'm not sure. The disaster part I get, but what perfect lie have I told?" Then her brain did that clicking thing. She looked up at Reed. *Perfect lies.* She had gotten the message after he had almost kissed her. What if whoever was behind the messages was actually trying to warn her? *What if the killer is Reed and he's only using you? You're the disaster.*

"You okay?" Reed asked, looking up at her with concern.

"Yeah." She took a sip of her tea. "Beth found an imprint or whatever garb she was talking. The gist of it, she's having to decode it due to blockers, but the main imprint was entangled in all the blockers." She had no idea what Beth had been talking about and had nodded along, doing her best to lend a listening ear. She was clueless when it came to the interworkings of computer codes. It was something she vowed to have Beth make her better at. In this computer-generated time, she needed to learn more than the basics. Books, however, would always be her number one love.

She told Reed she would call him later and thanked him for dinner. As she was leaving, she glanced back over her shoulder. Reed was on his phone, smiling at the screen. *Are you up to something?*

The thought stayed with her as she pulled into the school's parking lot. It stayed with her as she took her seat and waited for Gary to show up. She hated the doubt lingering inside of her, but she couldn't deny it. He had said he was intrigued by her, but why? There was nothing intriguing about Nora. She was a hermit. There was nothing thrilling about her.

"Hey," Stacey said, sitting down beside her. "What do you think today's meetings about? We don't have another competition for six weeks."

Disbelief flooded through Nora. Had Gary not mentioned the varsity meet to the group? It would figure. Gary hated confrontations, which was another reason she didn't think he was the puppet master. He was notorious for putting bad news off until the last minute. But this? This was going to be a blow to so many of the team members. Varsity only aimed at the top two debaters on a team. It didn't matter what grade they were in or how long they had been on the team. What mattered were their scores. As it stood, Gary and Nora were a clear choice. They outranked the others without question.

Stacey would be the one to take it the hardest. As someone who wanted to go into politics, she thrived at trying to make the top scores. If the varsity competition was to take the top three, she would be on board. As it was, she wasn't. A varsity title would look killer on a scholarship application, as everyone knew. Once she realized what it meant and that she wasn't going to compete, she would be crushed.

Nora glanced back over her shoulder to find Stacey's mom sitting in the back. At least Stacey would have support once the meeting was over. Nora couldn't believe Gary would do this to them. Why hadn't he said something before?

As Gary took the stage, anger burned through Nora. She was tired of secrets and lies, and here she was, witnessing the outcome of yet another secret. The team was going to be crushed, all because Gary hadn't prepped the others, as was his job, months ago.

"Thank you all for coming," Gary started as he looked out over the crowd.

Nora wasn't sure what came over her, but she found herself rushing to the stage. Gary eyed her, unsure of what she was doing. Nora never took to speaking in front of the team. That was all on Gary. Too bad Gary had failed this time.

"Hey, guys," Nora said. Her hands were slick with sweat and the microphone she had grabbed off the stage floor slid down, causing her to almost drop it. Nervous laughter bubbled out of her chest. "As you all know I don't do this," she said, gesturing to the microphone. "There's no opponent or bribe for standings." The others chuckled, getting her debate ranking joke. She sobered up, knowing what she was about to say wasn't going to go over well. "I wanted to step up here and show that I'm not going to cower down and pretend like what Gary is about to tell you is okay. Our team has already been through enough with the accusations floating around town." Okay, most of the accusations were aimed at her, but that was beside the point. "Gary and I neglected this team, so I'm going to stand here with him and take the brunt of your anger with him." *I shouldn't have to*, she wanted to say but refrained. She was no less to blame than Gary. She could have said something, could have encouraged him to push the team to do better if they wanted to make varsity, but she'd stayed quiet and left it for him to deal with. It's what she was good at. That was on no one but herself, which was why she was taking the stand now to show them she was sorry. It was too little too late for them, but her cowering in the third row would only make it worse.

She noticed Amy Hollis had come closer, now only a few rows behind Stacey. She was tense and looked to her daughter in concern. Sympathy poured out of Nora for her. She was going to have to console an inconsolable daughter in less than ten minutes. All because her president and vice president had failed her.

Gary went on to tell the team about the varsity competition. As he did, she realized something. It was from the way Gary kept apologizing and saying these things happen. These things don't happen, they're planned. Gary had planned on this. He had wanted that varsity spot and didn't want to fight for it. If Stacey had known, she would have pushed and put in more time. She would have demanded that he let her take the stage more. This way, the way of not telling them, had left him cruising in the lead.

Once he was finished, Stacey stormed out of the room, along with Beth Ann. Brittany and the others sat there, staring up at Gary in shock. Amy Hollis glared up at Gary and Nora before chasing her daughter down in the parking lot. She wasn't sure if she imagined it or not, but she felt Amy had directed her angry glare more at her than Gary. Perhaps it was because she thought Nora was supposed to be Stacey's friend.

When everyone had slowly trickled out of the auditorium, defeated and pissed off, Nora turned on Gary. "How could you have done this?"

"Me?" He laughed. Nora glared at him. Was he laughing at her? "What about you, Ms. Perfect? You knew our league was up for varsity this year but in the last six months you didn't say one word. Don't lay this on me."

She stepped closer to him. "There's a difference between you and me. I didn't say anything because I'm selfish and keep to myself. You didn't say anything because you're selfish and wanted the title for yourself. Had I thought about it, I would have said something." She made a wide gesture over the now empty auditorium. "They all deserved a shot at this."

"What are you going to do about it now, princess? You going to throw up a white flag and forfeit?" The arrogance in his tone made her sick.

"That's exactly what I'm going to do." He called out after her, but she ignored him. She wasn't going to give him the time of day. Look where letting him take the lead had gotten them, snarls and disgrace.

Before backing out of the parking lot, she caught sight of Amy and Stacey parked three slots over. Stacey was huddled over in her mother's arms, crying. Amy was doing her best to console her daughter, but after a blow like that, nothing was going to soothe the betrayal. Not today anyway.

By the time she got home, she was exhausted. She'd been full of apprehension and excitement when leaving earlier. Now, she didn't care if she ever left again. She was quite sure Reed was behind Kyle and Ryan's murders somehow. Gary was a prick. And her time put in the debate team could all be over at the snap of her fingers.

She pulled up the email for Mr. Alvearies once her laptop fired up. Beth laid sprawled across Nora's bed, still sorting through code, while Nora started thirteen different emails to which she deleted them all. A part of her didn't want to quit the debate team. It was the only thing she truly enjoyed about school. The competition. The fight to be better at delivering the facts so as to persuade the crowd.

By 10:30 she gave up. She needed more time to think rather than fly off the handle and delete a part of her life she loved. Beth scooted to the end of the bed as Nora piled up under the covers. She didn't look inclined to go anywhere.

"Are you going to sleep there all night?" Nora draped her arm over her face, ready to block out this day.

"Maybe," Beth grumbled. "I'm so close to cracking this it's making me sick."

Nora's phone vibrated on her nightstand. She had two messages, one from Liv and one from Reed.

Reed: Pick one: The Hobbit, Star Wars, or Harry Potter.

Liv: Call me. I miss you.

She ignored Reed's message and called Liv. Considering she still didn't know where she stood with him and the dire desperation in Liv's message, she was going to be the good friend she wanted to be. The person she needed to be. She was starting to learn, by hiding herself from the world all this time, she had done nothing but damage herself.

She and Liv talked for a while about school and nothing in particular. Charlie still wasn't talking to her. She claimed she needed more time to process everything that happened. Nora couldn't blame her. She was still trying to figure out the whos, whys, and whats of it all herself. Still, she couldn't believe Charlie was blaming Liv of all people.

That's what fear will do to you. It tears your mind apart until you believe the unbelievable. The thought made her think of Reed.

"I hate to say it, but I miss our meetups," Liv said. Nora related. Even with everything going on, she still thought about meeting up with Liv and Charlie at the library. "Maybe when this is all over we can start over."

"Hopefully," Nora answered, though they both knew it was a lie. They were scarred, damaged from the reality of what could happen even in a make-believe world.

"Stay safe, Nora," Liv warned. "This is far from over."

The warning sent a chill down Nora's spine as she ended the call. She knew it was far from over. What she feared was where it would go before it was all over.

"Have you talked to Reed tonight?" Beth asked, her focus still on her laptop.

Nora picked at a lose thread on her ancient sweater. It was once her mom's, back when she was in college. "No," Nora answered, not really wanting to emphasize further. What did it matter to Beth anyway?

"You should," she said, still not looking at Nora.

Her fascination stayed with the thread. *How did they weave so many small threads together like this?* She briefly glanced at her phone. The unanswered text screaming at her.

"Nora," Beth snapped. She sat up from her computer to give Nora her full attention. "Why wouldn't you talk to him?"

Nora's stomach twisted and she bit down on her lip. *Because I'm afraid of him.* "I don't know if I can trust him."

This was the last thing Beth had been expecting to hear. Her faced scrunch up. "Why can't you trust him? Everything about him screams safety."

Nora rolled over on her side, not wanting to look at Beth. If there was one thing she could be real with Beth about, it was this. "I keep asking myself why. Why now? It kind of feels like he's just... setting me up or something."

Beth let out a disgusted groan. She climbed over Nora and laid down next to her sister so they were face-to-face. "You're an idiot, you know that?" Nora opened her mouth to defend herself, but Beth slapped a warm hand over her lips. "He is head over heels crazy about you."

"He's only that way because he wants something from me. I just don't know what it is." She had been mulling over it all day but couldn't figure out why he would choose her to set up for murder of all people. What did she have to offer him? Money? He could have done that with any of the kids at Pinewood. She knew why. She was the easiest target. The weakest link.

"Oh, I don't know, Nora. Perhaps it's your bubbling speculative personality." Beth wrapped her arms around her sister and pulled her closer. "If only you could see it."

"See what?"

"The way he looks at you," Beth whispered. "It's the way every girl dreams of being looked at."

Nora's heart hitched. She feared what Beth had to say, how it would pierce her heart and make whatever was to come next unbearable. "How's that?"

"As if you are the moon. You shine brighter to him than all the rest. He looks at you with wonder as he plans his next adventure." Her breath was a hot whisper against Nora's ear. "You're his wild moon woman."

That night, Nora dreamed of open roads and wide spaces as the moon shone bright in the sky above.

Chapter Eighteen

Mr. Fuller was droning on about the structure of a pinecone and its importance to photosynthesis when Nora's name was called over the intercom. Mr. Fuller looked agitated at the interruption and told her to hurry as she gathered her things. She'd never been so happy to be pulled from a class in all her life. Mr. Fuller wasn't typically full of life but today proved to be difficult for him. His tone was an octave lower, giving him that perfect boring as hell teacher title.

On her way to the office, her phone vibrated in her backpack. Sidestepping between two rows of lockers, she hurried to pull it out. She'd been waiting to hear from Liv all day. Charlie had showed up at her house in the middle of the night, bawling and demanding answers. Charlie's brother hadn't just lost a best friend. Charlie had lost so much more. She'd been in love with Ryan and couldn't get past that blinding pain to see that Liv had nothing to do with it, not until she'd collapsed in Liv's arms a sobbing mess.

She was disappointed to find it was a message from Beth.

Beth: What do you think it's about this time?

Disgruntled, Nora started to put her phone away when it vibrated with another incoming text.

Reed: Keep me updated.

There was one comfort out of all this, she wasn't going at it alone. Beth had stayed up most of the night trying to decode all the interface put into the block for the unknown number. She was determined to crack it and find the jerkhole sending them. During breakfast, Reed had texted her to ask if she was okay. It was nice having a few people in her corner. The sucky part was the unknown. She still couldn't shake the question of Reed's trust.

Her dad stood in the office doorway, smiling and talking to Mrs. Vass. The secretary laughed at whatever he said before Nora walked inside, cutting off the joke. "Ah, here she is," Mrs. Vass said, still red from laughter.

"Nora," her dad drawled and then thanked the secretary before escorting her out of the office. Once they were outside, the pleasant smile he'd held in place vanished and he tucked his hands into his coat.

"Dad, what's going on?" she asked, wary. She didn't like the heavy look in his eyes.

"I wish I was here under better circumstance," he said, his jaw tightening as he looked across the grounds. Nora followed his gaze to find a police officer watching them. It was a run of the mill school security officer. "The police are wanting to question you. I told Donald what you told me about the two girls." Nora's heart seized up until she remembered Donald was her dad's lawyer. "He advised that you come clean about your relationship with these girls."

The way he said relationship made Nora cut her eyes up at him. "Friendship, you mean."

He rubbed his hands down his face. "I hope, for your sake, that that title stays true during all this." The car beeped as he hit the button to unlock the doors. "It doesn't look good," he added as they settled inside his sleek black Mercedes.

Nora went on the defensive. She was still confused as to whether or not to believe Liv and Charlie had anything to do with what was happening, but she wasn't about to let her father – or anyone – throw suspicion at them based on the status quo. "If this has anything to do with where they live, you can let that go. It isn't fair⬚"

"Nora," her father snapped, "how dare you insinuate such a thing. This has nothing to do with status or money. It's about murder, Nora. Murder! No amount of money or a street address matters when it comes to that and people buckle when they get scared, no matter who they are. That is my point."

Shame flurried through her. "But you've always pushed and sheltered me and Beth away from the west side."

Her father sighed and seemed to deflate. "Honey, it has nothing to do with money or housing or even the people, well, most of the people. I pushed you because I didn't want you to get lazy. I've worked hard for what we have, came from nothing. I wanted to encourage you, push you to what I know you can be, because no one was there to do the same for me." He signaled to turn on Elm and waited for the light to change. His hands tightened on the steering wheel. "I hate that you think so little of me."

Guilt rammed into Nora and she wanted to run and hide. "Dad, I'm sorry. It's just… you sheltered us so much and never seemed interested to talk about town culture."

He turned into the police station's parking lot. His face was grim as he cut the engine and looked out at the two-story building. "That's because I missed it and I didn't know how to balance the life I wanted for you two and the life I used to live."

Nora rested her hand over his on the console. "I'm sorry, Dad." He patted her hand. With a tight smile, he got out of the car and led her inside. To her relief, Liv and Charlie weren't there. Detective Taylor and Garcia were though, and they didn't bat an eyelash at Nora's fear. They'd been through this routine enough to push aside any qualms a suspect might have. Their empathy was long gone.

After two hours of grueling questions, Nora and her dad walked out of the police station. Nora wiped the sweat off her brow, a sense of calm settling in on her. She'd handled that like she would any debate. The questions were all mostly the same, yet they tried tripping her up by asking in a different manner. It didn't matter. Facts were facts and as long as you held true to them, no one could change the truth.

The only time she had almost faltered was when Garcia mentioned Liv, Charlie, and Reed. *Do you not find the circumstances a bit too coincidental? Do you not see that you are the only connection between Reed and the school, Liv and Charlie, with a mix of the debate team? Nora, you're standing right in the middle of it all.* She had felt her dad tense next to her, but she'd kept her cool. She'd answered Garcia's questions with facts, not theories. Theories were all the police had to go on right now. They had no solid evidence.

Nora's phone chimed and she looked down to see it was a message from Reed.

Reed: Everything okay?

She smiled at the screen, but guilt twisted in her gut. There was a part of her that still didn't trust him. It was that small part that didn't trust anyone. Someone close to her, someone who knew her, was playing fiddle with Nora's emotions. They knew how to get to her, knew secrets about her, but were unwilling to show their face. Why? What were they waiting for? Why were they hiding? Was Reed keeping tabs on her to get information and see how his tactics were toying with her life? The doubt was eating her alive.

Choosing not to answer him, she pocketed her phone.

"Where to kiddo?" her dad asked as he slid into the driver seat.

Nora glanced at her phone. "School's almost out," she murmured with relief. She needed to see Liv and Charlie but wasn't sure how her parents would take it, considering the investigation. A plan formed and she swallowed the guilt she felt. One more lie. It was only one more lie. "Do you mind if I take the car and go meet up with Gary? I'd kind of like to get busy with varsity preparations and get my mind off all this." She was playing his worry and could tell it was working. It ate her up inside.

"Of course, honey."

The trees and hum of the town became a blur as Nora looked out the window, lost in her thoughts. She'd studied law and it entailed to know that going to meet up with Liv and Charlie right now was not the best of ideas. It would set up suspicions and with the eyes heavy on them, they didn't need that kind of attention right now. But they were also her friends. As hung up as she was on her doubt, she also needed to check and make sure they were okay. Liv had sounded worried that morning as she told Nora about Charlie showing up at her house. The deeper they got into this, the more Nora was starting to believe Liv and Charlie had nothing to with what happened with Kyle. She felt sick for even having thought about it to begin with.

That admission only left one conclusion... Reed. He'd been on the outer fringes of her life, Charlie's life, and Liv's. There was no one else interested enough in her life right now, other than Reed, who had come out of nowhere and snagged her attention after Kyle's death. That's when she had discovered his frequent trips to the library. That he was friends with Charlie's brothers and that he lived close to them.

She thought about their talks and how he made her laugh. She loved talking with him. It was easy. She was lying to herself when she said she didn't care. She did care. She didn't want him to be behind this. The small ache in her chest told her everything she needed to know, she was starting to fall for him. *You're his wild moon woman.* The hot flare of tears building burned her eyes, but she fought to push them back. If it turned out he was the one behind all of this, she knew her heart would break. It already was. Distance, it was the only thing she could do from here on out to protect herself.

As if he was sensing her thoughts about him, her phone dinged with a message from him.

Reed: Can we talk?

The tears started to build again, but she shoved it aside and closed the screen. She prayed with everything inside of her that she was wrong, but until proven otherwise, she had to do whatever it took to keep him at bay. If he was behind this, she wasn't going to continue to give him a free show.

As if sensing her pain through their sisterly bond, a text pinged in from Beth.

Beth: You okay?

Before she could answer another message popped up.

Beth: I've got some information for you.

The thought of Beth hunched over her laptop last night twisted Nora's insides. She shouldn't have included her in all this. Beth was fragile and Nora didn't want to be the cause of a spiral into the dark abyss. The emotions of the day were catching up to Nora and she put her phone away, too overwhelmed to reply.

"Everything okay, pumpkin?" her dad asked as he pulled into the driveway. Nora looked up at their house with a longing to run to her room and hide.

"Fine," she answered, unable to look at him. "Do you mind if I take your car? I get nervous driving moms." It was also more convenient for her considering the keys were within her reach.

Her father looked down at the keys jingling from his fingers. His hold tightened on them for a second, indecision tight on his face. With a sigh, he handed them over. "Be back by seven. I think we could all use a bit of family fun tonight."

Nora smiled. "Family Feud?"

"I was thinking Monopoly."

The smile fell off her lips and she groaned. "You always win, and Mom gets mad."

"Precisely," he said with a smirk. "I like when your mom gets mad."

Nora fake gagged. "Dad," she groaned. "TMI."

He chuckled, and as Nora walked around the car to get in the driver seat, he paused to give her a hug. "I love you, Nora Bear."

Nora's arms tightened around his waist. "I love you too, Dad."

Getting in the car, she pulled out her phone and sent Liv a quick message. While she waited for her reply, she adjusted the seats and mirrors. Her dad's six-foot frame too much for her five-foot-two. She could barely reach the peddles. When her phone dinged, she picked it up to read Liv's reply.

Liv: Yeah, we're at my house. Coming by?

She typed out a quick confirmation and then backed out the driveway. A small ray of cheer beamed through her as she turned toward town. She needed to see her friends, now more than ever. She'd never understood the importance of friendship, had always played it down as unimportant, until now. All those years she'd only been lying to herself to ease the pain of loneliness. This was what friendship was about. Going to talk and ease the worry hidden so deep inside. She also realized it could have been her sister all along, but she was too cautious with Beth. She'd vowed three years ago to never put Beth through the turmoil she had before, no matter how bad she was hurting. Beth didn't need to worry.

Now, having two friends she could lean on – even just a little bit – spoke volumes to her. A pang of longing stirred her thoughts as Reed came to mind, but she shoved it away, hard. She could not go there. He was not someone she could lean on.

She was halfway across town when her phone chimed.

Gary: I need to talk to you. Can you meet me at the auditorium? It's important.

Could she? She knew what he wanted to talk about, and personally, she didn't want to deal with it right now. She had other things to worry about than some stupid debate and his hurt feelings. Gary was persistent, though, and she didn't want to have to deal with him at school in front of everyone tomorrow. He didn't care about causing a scene. If it was for his purposes, he was good with it.

Sighing, she hit the audio command and replied with **I'll be there in 10.**

She did a block around downtown and headed back for the school. She was going to make this quick. There was nothing he could say to make her change the way she felt. She'd said what she said and wasn't going to back down. Gary had done the team wrong by waiting until the last minute to tell everyone about varsity. He deserved to feel like shit about it for a few days. She doubted he would. Gary never felt like shit about anything.

After parking in the school lot, she sent a quick text to Liv to let her know she was meeting up with Gary at the school and that it shouldn't take long. On her way inside, her phone chimed. She glanced down, figuring it was a text from Liv. Her stomach tightened when she saw who it was. It was Reed.

Reed: I just talked to Beth. She's worried. I'm worried. Please don't dodge us. We only want to help.

Beth had called Reed? She started to call her sister, ashamed for making her worry. A loud bang from inside caught her attention and she pocketed her phone. She would call Beth after she settled this thing with Gary. She was more than ready to get this over with and head over to Liv's. If it turned out Beth needed her, she'd just go home. But first, Gary would have to be dealt with.

The halls were quiet, and an uneasy feeling came over her. She'd been down these halls a hundred times when no one else was around. It was nothing new. Why the sudden quake of fear now? She shook off the feeling, blaming it on her nerves and the overwhelming emotions catching up to her.

Inside the auditorium, the room was dark except for a single light shining down on the microphone set in the middle of the stage. She heard the door behind her click and she jumped, a cold chill spreading over her.

Where was Gary?

A blue screen hanging on the back wall of the stage lit up. Nora's stomach dropped as a message was typed out, each letter a jab to her heart. She held her breath and once the message was finished, her heart beat against her chest so hard, her breath shallow, she was sure she'd pass out.

Welcome, Nora. Ready for a debate?

Chapter Nineteen

Nora's heart pounded as she beat against the door and screamed for help. She knew the building was empty but there was always that off chance. Maybe someone had come back for something they forgot. Maybe the janitor had stayed late. Either way, she wasn't giving in to defeat that easy.

A loud bang came from behind the stage and Nora dunked down between the seats. Panic clawed at her chest and throat, making it almost impossible to breathe. Trying to pull herself together, she took a few deep breaths and laid her head against the cool metal of the seat's backing. The cool touch helped bring her back and calm her nerves. She was grounded and safe… for now.

She pulled out her phone to find she had no service. *How is that possible?* she wondered. She always had service inside the auditorium. It was how she survived ninety percent of the assemblies and all of the student council meetings. A flashing red light above the door caught her attention. It was a wireless signal jammer. She recognized it thanks to the ones they put up during debates at some schools. Nora's panic began to pound again. This person wasn't going to let her out of here alive.

A repetitive click echoed from the front of the amphitheater, the click setting Nora's nerves on edge. She reached for the back of the chair, fully prepared to look over the top to see what was happening, but then froze.

What if the person had a gun? They'd blow her top off. Her phone fell down her lap and onto the floor. *Of course,* she wanted to scream but kept it to herself. No need making things easier for the killer.

Holding up her phone, she opened the camera and turned it to front facing. She could see the stage perfectly. The red curtains pulled almost shut, except for where the podium stood in the middle with a bright light displaying it. In the back, the screen was still lit up with her name and the challenge for a debate.

Red heels darted across the screen but before Nora could focus on them, they were gone. As she searched the auditorium, her mind raced with who it could be. Who did she know who wanted her dead and always wore heels? The answer was there, scratching at her brain. She could feel it but no matter how hard she tried she couldn't grasp it.

A figure came across Nora's camera seconds later. As the person stormed up the aisle, their face hot with anger, Nora's blood ran cold. She pushed herself back as far as she could, her mind unable to grasp the reality of what was about to happen. Seconds later, Amy Hollis stopped at the end of the aisle and set her sights on Nora. Her glare was shocking compared to the sweet smile she often held in place, her perfectly manicured hands rested on her hips.

"Why, hello, Nora. It's such a pleasure to have you." She stepped into the row. "I'm sorry for the rush, but with varsity coming up, I knew I had to do something rash. The police around here like to drag ass when anything remotely exciting happens. It's the only action they ever get." She stopped inches away from Nora, her usual pleasant smile in place.

Nora pushed back, though it did no good. What was she hoping would happen, the floor would swallow her? "Why?" she managed to stammer.

Pain shot through Nora's scalp and she cried out as Amy pulled her up by her hair and began leading her down the aisle. "I'll tell you why, sweet cheeks. Because I'm tired of my Stacey getting overlooked in life. Her father picked that skanky salon lady over his own daughter. Her grandparents always choose those snotty kids of my sisters. At school, you or Gary always take the spotlight. I wasn't having it anymore. You don't deserve to hog the spotlight every time." She gave Nora's hair a hard yank.

Nora cried out and tried clawing at Amy's hand to loosen her grip, but it did no good. "Why didn't she say something?"

Amy laughed, dry and harsh. "Like that would have done any good. Gary would never replace you, not willingly anyway. It's why I decided to start this whole scheme." She paused when they reached the front. "You know, I have you to thank."

"Me?" Nora said, her voice barely audible. Pain seared through her scalp as Amy tightened Nora's hair around her fist. Nora cursed herself for not taking that defensive class Beth had wanted her to take a few months ago. "What did I do?" Her voice was shaky, but she had to keep Amy talking until she devised a plan to get out of this. At the moment, she had nothing. Amy had done a good job cleaning the place up and taking away all possible weapons. The streamer that had been across the front of the stage front earlier was even gone.

"You're little murder groupies. It was just the thing I needed. Figuring out how to murder someone isn't as easy as you think." She glared down at Nora and what she saw scared her. There was nothing, no life left, no remorse. "I'm not surprised a girl like you would create a twisted group like that. The weird ones always have the good secrets."

"How did you know?" Nora had always been sure she was careful. If she saw a familiar face at the library, she was out. She'd always lived in fear of what others thought of her and how they would react to her little club. They'd think she was crazy. They wouldn't see it as a mystery game like so many others. Look where that fear had got her, in the hands of a real murderer.

"You think you're sneaky, but Stacey tells me everything. She told me how odd you have been acting. How you've been sneaking around on Thursdays. You think no one is watching you, but someone is always watching, Nora. Always." Amy stopped in front of the stage and spun Nora around to face her. "I've been following you for a while. I wanted to kill you a long time ago, but then second guessed that decision and thought, 'What if I framed her?' The shame, oh, I knew it would eat you alive. The same way the disregard has eaten my poor Stacey away for years. It was a good setup, but the police are taking too long to piece it all together. With varsity around the corner, it's time for me to take matters into my own hands."

The fire that lit in Amy's eyes was the only warning Nora was given before her head was thrust to the side with force. Pain exploded in the side of her head right behind her ear. A trickle of liquid ran down her neck, tickling her skin. *Blood,* her brain registered seconds before her head was being lifted up and slammed back into the corner of the stage floor. Words. She heard words but couldn't register what they meant as her body slumped to the hard, cold floor.

~

Nora blinked several times against the bright light shining down on her. The glow illuminated the red curtains surrounding the stage. Looming over her was the projector screen with a new message. *The debate is over.* Adrenaline pumped through her. She knew what that message meant. Game over for her.

The click of Amy's heels was Nora's only warning she was close, but her head still pounded. She couldn't distinguish where exactly Amy was. Not willing to go down without a fight, she rushed up on her feet, her fists swinging wild. Her vision swam, the injury to her head too much for her. Amy laughed and caught Nora by the arm.

"You are the dramatic one, always have loved the spotlight," Amy sneered.

"Hate it," Nora mumbled, still trying to get her bearings. *Why are there two floors?*

"Now," Amy continued as if Nora hadn't spoken at all, "comes the time for your big finale."

Panic helped clear away the fog when Nora saw the noose. It was positioned behind the podium where a camera was set up and ready. Nora swung out and brought her elbow up but made no connection. She was still groggy, her movements slow.

Amy looked down at her watch. "Don't worry, sweetie. That sedative I gave you should kick in any moment now." She sat Nora down in a chair under the noose.

Nora felt heavy. *Sedative!* She jerked up out of the chair. *I have to escape.* Something hard hit her in the back of the head, right on the blow she'd taken earlier. Still, she tried to stand. When the gun came into view, she froze. Amy stood before her now, a handgun pointed in her face. "I'm not above shooting you. It won't change a thing."

Numb, Nora sat back down. Defeat started to set in her mind. *She's going to win. I'm defenseless. This is it for me.* The reality of that truth made a tear slip down her cheek. She didn't want to give in to this. She wanted to fight, but her body felt so heavy. The possibility of survival seemed mute.

Another tear slipped down her cheek and she picked up her head to stare out over the empty seats. She'd always known her final day of being behind that podium would come. She'd just never imagined it would come like this. With her being murdered rather than taking one final bow before walking out the door to a bright future. That bright future was looking dim now.

A gavel, tucked under the lip of the podium, snagged her attention. Her vision was still blurry, but she could still make it out just fine. Amy was busy adjusting a rope around her right leg as a plan formed in her mind. She could lurch forward, grab the gavel, and swing fast at Amy's temple. It was a solid plan. There was only one problem. She wasn't going to be fast enough. She tried raising her hand, but it felt heavy. How was she supposed to get to the gavel?

Drowsiness started to take over her mind, but she fought it. She had to get to the gavel.

A loud bang came from behind her and Amy stood, alarmed. She held her gun out in front of her while Nora struggled to hold her head up. *The gavel.* It was her focus. Amy walked off behind her, her attention on whatever Nora couldn't see.

This is my chance. Nora leaned forward and went to stand, but the floor came closer rather than moving farther away. Her hand twisted underneath her at an awkward angle as she hit the floor. Her face slammed against the rough texture.

A gunshot blasted through the air, but Nora was far too gone to care. She became lost in oblivion.

~

"Hey, sleepy head," Reed said as he came into the room carrying a balloon.

Nora chuckled as she read the *Get Well* message. "You know, they're fixing to send me home."

Reed gave her a cheeky grin. "I know, but I figured you needed something to remember your hero."

"Is that so?" She resisted the urge to scratch at the bandage wrapped around her head. The medical wrap was uncomfortable to say the least. "I think I'm going to have a hard time forgetting him, with or without the balloon."

"That so?" he asked, resting his arms on the edge of her bed as he leaned in closer. "I'm glad you're okay and going home. When I found you on that stage…"

Nora rested her hand on his. "Let's not talk about it. We all have our regrets and moments we wish we could forget from the last few weeks. The only thing we can do is learn from it, forgive, and move on." She'd been the first to start throwing out apologies once she came to and saw her friends and family gathered around her. She'd doubted them all for one reason or another and wanted them all to know how sorry she was. She should have never let her insecurities cause such a rift between her and those who cared about her.

Reed squeezed her hand. "They're moving Amy to the state prison tomorrow. Stacey is going to stay with her father."

"As much as I dislike Amy Hollis right now, I hope her dad pulls his head out of his ass and treats Stacey right." Stacey had been heavy on her mind since she woke up and heard the full story about Amy and her plan to take her daughter to the top. She'd done it all for her daughter.

After waking up in the hospital, surrounded by her family, Nora had known she was lucky but confused as to how they had found her in time. Her mother had been the one to fill her in with the details. Beth had been suspicious about Amy after finding an inscription with Amy's name encrypted in the code. When Reed called her, concerned about Nora, Beth let her suspicions be known. The two took quick action and tracked Nora's phone to the last location recorded. When Reed found the auditorium locked, he went through a hidden room in the back. He'd once been a stagehand for the drama club and knew all the hidden nooks behind the stage. Amy had taken a shot at him but missed. He was able to subdue her until Detective Taylor and Detective Garcia showed up.

Amy confessed later that she'd orchestrated the whole scheme in order to get her daughter ahead. She'd first chosen Kyle after getting home from eavesdropping on Nora at her meeting. Stacey had told her mom about the confrontation with Nora that day in the hallway. Stacey had felt Nora was shucking her responsibilities as vice president. That's when her mother took it upon herself to do something. She'd later chosen Ryan, wanting to draw attention to Nora's connection to Liv and Charlie. It had all been well thought out, but there were flaws in almost every plan. Lucky for Nora, Amy's flaw happened to be her discrediting the love and care Reed and Beth had for Nora. If it hadn't been for them and their worry, she'd be six feet under instead of in a hospital bed.

After one final checkup by the doctor, Nora was discharged. She said goodbye to Reed before leaving, with a promise to call him later. Reluctant, he let her go after her dad gave him a stern look. He was adamant about her getting her rest. She'd laughed but smiled back at Reed as she was wheeled around the corner and out of his sight.

Beth was waiting for her in her room once she got home. Without saying a word, Beth scooted over on the bed and made room for Nora. They snuggled close together and sighed.

"I'm glad you're okay," Beth whispered as they snuggled there in the dark.

Nora's throat grew tight with emotion. If it hadn't been for Reed and Beth, she knew she wouldn't be there to hear her sister say that. Shame filled her as she looked over at her sister and she thought about the way she'd treated her the last three years. "I'm sorry," she whispered.

"For what?"

"For always trying to shield you. I always think of you as this fragile person, but you're not. You're stronger than I give you credit for." Her eyes filled with tears, making Beth blurry. "You're so much stronger than I am."

Beth snuggled in closer and wrapped Nora in a hug. "I'm only strong because of you. You are my rock and I know I wouldn't be where I am if not for you."

Hugging it out, which took a while, Nora finally pulled away a little and playfully pushed Beth's shoulder. "Hey, you're pretty savvy with all that computer coding. You ever thought about pursuing it?"

"Actually," Beth said, reaching over to grab her phone. "I've made an app for you."

"Seriously?" Nora sat up, intrigued. "For me?"

Beth blushed. "Well, I mean, anyone can use it once it goes live but I made it for you. It's a murder mystery app. The chat room you were using was okay, but this let's you create the mysteries and then other people can try to solve it. It's a time challenge."

Nora took Beth's phone and started investigating. There were different roles you could play, coins you could collect for clues, along with levels you could reach to earn badges. It was impressive. "This is amazing, Beth. I'm so proud of you."

"Thanks." Beth played with the cover, not seeming to care about the app.

"What's wrong?" Nora asked.

"It's nothing," she mumbled, but when Nora gave her a stern look, she sighed. "It's just, well, I heard Mom and Reed talking about your recent panic attacks. They also said something about you being afraid of being like me."

Nora's blood ran cold and she set the phone down. "Beth, it has nothing to do with you. It's just... I like being in control and when I'm like that, I'm not in control. It scares me."

Beth wouldn't meet her eyes. "It scares me too."

Nora knew she had to fix this, be the big sister to admit when she was wrong and let her sister know there was nothing wrong with being who you are. Because in all honesty, there was nothing truly wrong with embracing who you are, even when it's not perfect and completely out of your control. It's life: Loud. Imperfect. Flawed. Extraordinary.

"And that's why we are going to beat this together. We will be there to support one another and talk each other off the self-destructive ledge. The first step is embracing it and then learning everything we can to control it. We may be a little flawed, but that doesn't make us broken. Maybe we can even start a support group and raise awareness. There's probably more people around here that suffers from the same thing, they just don't talk about it because they don't understand it."

That perked Beth up. "You think so?"

"Oh, you know it. Have you ever seen the way Tiffany Newsby bites her lip and always looks around with worried eyes before answering a question? Or how about Mrs. Lang down the street? She's always keeping her head down, unsure of herself. They just need someone to stand up and say I'm here for you, even if you just need someone to sit in silence with."

They talked for hours after that about the possibilities, including getting their mother involved to make cookies for their future group meetings. After Beth fell asleep, Nora stared at the ceiling, wide-awake and oddly thankful for what Amy had done. Yes, she'd taken it too far by killing Ryan and Kyle, but she'd brought some good into Nora's life from her antics. She'd brought to life so much that Nora had suppressed. Now that it had been brought to life, Nora was surer about her future than she had ever been.

Life wasn't perfect. In fact, it was a beautiful mess and Nora intended to live every day with intention.

Six Months Later

Reed tossed the last luggage bag into the trunk while Nora hugged her sister. "I can't believe Mom is letting you go to New York City," she whispered in Beth's ear as she tightened her arms.

Beth chuckled. "You said that last night."

"That's because I can't believe it." She pulled back and smiled. "I'm not going to lie, I'm a little jealous."

"Why? You're going to Florida."

"Yeah, but I'm going to college. I'm eighteen. You're fifteen and going to a technical school, so unfair." She picked up her backpack off the ground and smiled at her sister. "But I'm happy for you. Promise to keep in touch?"

"I don't know… I could be pretty busy." Beth paused and then came in to hug Nora again. "I'll call every day."

"You better." Nora adjusted the necklace around Beth's neck. She wore an identical one. "Charlie meeting you there or are you guys picking her up?" After everything calmed down and everyone tried to get some piece of their life back together, Charlie and Beth really took off with the murder mystery app. When Beth mentioned going to a technical school in New York City, Charlie had applied for a scholarship to finish out her senior year. She'd been accepted and had already started taking classes online. Classes that didn't even count. That was passion.

"She's meeting us there. Her whole family is driving her down tomorrow."

Nora laughed. "That will be something to remember."

After Beth and her mom left for the long drive to New York City, Nora's dad got into the car to wait for her. She turned to Reed, not knowing how to say goodbye. Over the last six months, they had become inseparable. They spent most of the summer at the lodge, picnicking by the lake, swimming, and gazing at the stars while they talked the hours away. Liv and Charlie had joined them on most trips. Liv was still shaken by what had happened and spent most of the summer photographing life around her. She held her first gallery during Art Walk at the end of summer. No one was quite sure where Liv would be going or when, but she was living her life the way she needed to right now.

Her chest tightened as she looked up at him. They'd both known this day was coming after she set her sights on the Criminal Justice and Psychology College in Florida. However, knowing didn't make it any easier.

"You better call me every day," she said, stepping closer to him.

"You better find me an apartment, woman." He smirked and she could see the struggle in his eyes not to reach out and grab her. Reed planned to come join her at the start of the spring semester, with plans of going into law. He wasn't prepared to follow in his mom and dad's footsteps completely, but he knew he had a calling to serve and protect. It was in his blood. He'd wanted to join Nora now, but after his grandmother had a stroke over the summer, he decided to stay and help out for as long as he could. He and his grandfather knew she wouldn't be around much longer and Reed wanted to get every second he could with her.

"You can sleep in a box with that attitude, mister."

No longer able to hold back, he reached out and pulled her into his arms. "Better be a big box," he whispered against her lips. Nora sighed and fell deeper into his arms.

She was unsure of what the future held, but for now, she was living with the best of intentions and loving every second of it.

About the Author

Brandy Nacole is the Best-Selling Author of *Deep in the Hollow* and *The Shadow World Trilogy*. She is an urban legend addict who also plays detective along with her favorite drama shows. She lives in the hollows of Arkansas with her husband, three fun-loving kids, and two lazy rescue dogs. To learn more about Brandy and her books, visit her at brandynacole.com, follow @authorbnacole on Twitter, or on Instagram at @brandy_nacole_.

Made in the USA
Coppell, TX
14 March 2020

16833251R00136